LEGACY OF GRACE

CATHARINE DOBBS

PROLOGUE

A Nurse for the Nurse

Spring 1865

"There we are, my Lady. That'll help you sleep," Mary Carruthers said, stepping back from the bedside, as her daughter, Grace, watched from the corner of the room.

"Thank you, Mary... that's very kind of you. I feel... oh, I feel so weak and helpless. The spirit is willing, but the flesh is weak. How feeble I am," Lady Edith Kelly replied.

She was a grand, aristocratic woman, always immaculately dressed–despite the illness which best her–and was sitting up in bed, with pearls around her neck, wrapped in a fox skin shawl, sipping the cup of tea Grace's mother had given her. The room was dimly lit, the curtains drawn across the window–despite the sunshine outside–and the drapes around the bed partially pulled across.

"Don't worry, my Lady. I'll keep you comfortable. But please, try to get some sleep," Grace's mother replied.

Lady Edith nodded.

"Is Grace there? Is she hiding in the shadows? Come closer, child. I want to see your pretty face," she said.

Grace stepped forward. She was not afraid of Lady Edith. She had grown up at Carshalton House, the Norfolk home of Lady Edith, where her mother had nursed the ailing aristocrat for the last seven years. She always accompanied her mother at this time of day, standing in the corner of the room, and watching as Lady Edith was nursed. Grace's mother was always gentle, and always kind. Lady Edith depended on her, and night and day, she was a companion to her.

"I'm here, Lady Edith," Grace said, stepping forward in the dim light.

Lady Edith raised her hand, trembling, as Grace's mother took the cup and saucer from her.

"Just for a moment, Grace," she said, nodding, as Grace stood at the bedside.

Lady Edith ran her fingers over Grace's face, smiling at her, as Grace stood dutifully before her. She was in the last vestiges of her life–a life of grandness lived amongst the upper echelons of aristocratic society. She was the daughter of a duke and never married. Carshalton House had been a gift from her brother on his inheritance of the dukedom, and Lady Edith was the last of the siblings, a distant cousin set to inherit the estate on her death.

"Dear child, what a sweet little thing you are. Your looks remind me of myself in my childhood. What happy days those were," she said, a wistful look coming over her face, as though the sight of Grace brought with it long forgotten memories.

"We should leave you to your rest, my Lady," Grace's mother said, touching Grace on the shoulder.

"Yes, I mustn't disobey orders, now," Lady Edith replied, giving a weak smile.

Grace leaned forward and kissed her on the cheek, and Lady Edith sighed and closed her eyes.

"I'll bring your tonic later, my Lady," Grace's mother said, and taking Grace's hand, she led her from the room.

Closing the door behind her, Grace's mother sighed.

"What's wrong, Mother?" Grace asked, looking up at her mother, who seemed tired.

"Oh... it's nothing. I'll be all right. I need to sit down, though," she said, leaning against the doorframe and closing her eyes.

This had happened several times before in recent months. Her mother had been overcome with fatigue and had taken to her bed. Her face was pale, her expression distant, and still she leaned against the doorframe as Grace squeezed her hand.

"I'll help you to bed, Mother," she said, but her mother shook her head.

"No... I've got too much to do. It's her ladyship who's unwell. Who nurses the nurse?" she said, giving a weak smile and taking a deep breath.

She straightened up, supporting herself on the doorframe, but looking as though she could collapse at any moment.

"Mother, you can't go on like this. I'm worried about you," Grace said.

She was only seven years old, but she had grown up around illness–Lady Edith was an invalid, and Grace's mother nursed her day and night. She would never get better, life slipping gently away from her, until eventually...

"You mustn't be worried about me, Grace. I'll be quite all right. There now, I feel much better. Come along. Let's go down to the kitchen and see if we can't persuade Mrs. Lewes to give us each one of those delicious scones she was making earlier," Grace's mother said.

Grace nodded, knowing there would be no persuading her otherwise. But it was always the same – a dizzy spell, an insistence on being well, and a gradual decline. Grace knew her mother would be in bed by the end of the day, and so she was.

"Tell her not to exert herself. She can't help being unwell–I know that well enough," Lady Edith said, when Grace took the tonic to her later that evening.

"She will... get better though, won't she?" Grace asked.

Her mother had refused the suggestion of the doctor.

"I'm a nurse. I don't need a doctor to tell me what I already know," she had said, and Grace had only been allowed to fetch her a bowl of soup from the kitchen and plump her pillows.

"Will any of us ever get better, Grace? Oh... I'm sorry. I know you're worried about your mother. I'm sure she'll regain her strength soon enough," Lady Edith replied, grimacing as she administered the tonic to herself.

Grace nodded. She did not know what was wrong with her mother, or how to make her better. She had always admired the way her mother took care of Lady Edith – she was an ever-reassuring presence and devoted to her duties.

"I... she won't listen to advice," Grace said, and Lady Edith laughed.

"No invalid ever listens to advice, Grace. We all know what's best for us – even if it's not. Let your mother rest for a few days. She'll be all right. Come and see me tomorrow, won't you?" she said, and Grace nodded.

As she closed the door of Lady Edith's bedroom, tears welled up in her eyes. Grace wanted her mother to be well–to seek help, even in her stubbornness. They had no other family, and Grace had never known her father–he had died when she was very young, or so her mother had told her.

"And if I lose my mother, what would become of me?" she thought to herself, for she could not imagine the likes of the housekeeper, Mrs. Parks, or any of the other servants taking kindly to the presence of an orphan.

Even Lady Edith could not be expected to extend her generosity in such a way, and Grace was gripped by a sudden fear for her future. She hurried towards her mother's bedroom, opening the door cautiously and peering inside. The bed was empty, the sheets pulled back in disarray.

"Mother?" Grace called out, but there was no response.

Gripped by a sudden terror, Grace turned back from the empty room, hurrying down the corridor, and calling for her mother at the top of her voice. Grace and her mother slept on the second floor, below the servant's corridor, and Grace slept on a cot at the end of the bed.

A nurse–like a governess–occupied a strange position in a household, not entirely above stairs, but not entirely below, either, and Grace now called out for Mrs. Parks, anxious to find her mother, who should not have been out of bed. She had grown weaker that afternoon, paler, more withdrawn. She had complained of a headache, and Grace had brought her soup and tea. But she would not hear of having the doctor sent for and had become almost aggressive at the suggestion.

"I don't need the quack," she had snapped, before Grace had taken Lady Edith her tonic.

"What's all this shouting about, Grace? What are you doing, running up and down the corridors like this?" Mrs. Parks exclaimed, as Grace encountered her on the stairs leading down to the kitchen.

"It's my mother, Mrs. Parks. I can't find her anywhere," Grace exclaimed.

Mrs. Parks tutted.

"Well, there's no need to keep shouting about it. She's probably downstairs with Mrs. Lewes," the housekeeper said.

Mrs. Parks had been the housekeeper at Carshalton House for as long as anyone could remember. Grace was scared of her–she was a fierce woman, quick to anger, with a pinched face, narrow nose, and high forehead. She always wore black, and the jangling keys hanging from her belt were a sign for Grace to hide lest she encounter her in a corridor or in the hallway.

"I'm sorry, Mrs. Parks, it's just..." Grace began, stammering her response, but at that moment, a scream echoed up from the kitchen below, along with the smashing of crockery, and Mrs. Parks gave an angry exclamation.

"Are we to wake the dead?" she exclaimed, hurrying down the stairs.

Grace followed, terrified as to what they would find, and as they came around the corner at the top of the landing above the kitchen corridor, a terrible sight met their eyes.

The cook, Mrs. Lewes, had dropped the dish she was carrying, the fragments of china scattered over the flagstone floor, and there, lying at the bottom of the stairs, her face expressionless, her eyes wide, and blood seeping from a wound to her head, was Grace's mother.

She was dead, and in that moment, Grace's life changed forever.

PART I

DOCTOR BERKLEY

"Jcan't be certain what was wrong with her. A condition of the mind, perhaps. You say she was regularly overcome, then seemed to rally, then deteriorate?" Doctor Berkley, the village physician, said.

Grace nodded. She was sitting next to Lady Edith's bed. The shock of her mother's sudden death had not yet sunk in.

Doctor Berkley had been summoned at once, but there had been nothing he could do, save to certify the death. Grace had watched as two of the gardeners had removed her mother's body from the foot of the kitchen stairs. The undertaker was also summoned to make the necessary arrangements.

"I wish she'd told me more. I knew she was having these dizzy spells, but... oh, she was my nurse, and yet it was she who needed nursing," Lady Edith said, shaking her head.

"I'm afraid I don't think there was anything to be done, Lady Edith. We still don't understand enough about medicine to make certain diagnoses. I fear your nurse was overcome by whatever illness had taken hold. No doubt she was stoical–I knew her a little, of course, and that was always my impression.

Perhaps she didn't want to know what was wrong with her," he said, shaking his head.

Lady Edith glanced at Grace.

"My poor child," she whispered, reaching out and placing her hand on Grace's shoulder.

Grace looked up at her, not knowing what to say or what to do. She felt overwhelmed by grief. Her mother was everything to her, and now she was gone.

"I miss her," Grace whispered, and Lady Edith gave a weak smile.

"Oh, Grace... I know you do, of course, you do–you loved her, and she loved you. She lived for you, but you mustn't worry. I'll look after you," she said, and Doctor Berkley looked up in surprise.

"Lady Edith, I... when a child's parents are dead, it's usual for them to be sent to–" he began, but Lady Edith interrupted him.

"I won't hear that word used, Doctor. Mary Carruthers was my nurse. She served me faithfully for many years, and I'm not about to abandon her only child to– no, I won't hear of it," Lady Edith said, and for that, Grace could at least feel a certain relief.

She had feared she would be put out of the house immediately, sent to an orphanage or poorhouse–the fate of orphans, just as Doctor Berkley suggested. He was a young man who had quite recently arrived in Carshalton.

Fresh faced and eager, a recent graduate of London medical school, he had come to the countryside for his first practice. He had been diligent in his ministrations to Lady Edith and was highly spoken of in the village. Even the curate, whose wife was something of a hypochondriac, thought well of him.

"Your charity does you service, Lady Edith. Such places are... not nice. But if you're willing to keep the child here, I'm sure you'll have your reward on another shore," he said, glancing at Grace with a reassuring smile.

"I've no thought to reward Doctor Berkley. Grace brings me

pleasure. She's a good child, but I wonder… the poor thing can't reside forever in sorrow, and I'm too weak to be anything more than a figurehead to her. Would you teach her to read?" Lady Edith asked.

Grace looked up with a puzzled expression on her face, momentarily distracted from her grief by this strange request. Doctor Berkley, too, seemed to think it odd, but he nodded, clearly wishing to humour his patron.

"To read, Lady Edith?" he said, and she nodded.

"That's what I said, Doctor Berkley. It'll help her, and it'll help me, too. Her mother often read to me, and without her, who else can I hope to do so?" Lady Edith asked.

Grace had often sat to hear her mother read to Lady Edith. She would read the Bible, or other pious texts, and sometimes Shakespeare, too. Grace knew all the stories by heart, but the thought of reading them for herself was something else. Her mother had begun to teach her, but she had only the rudiments, and the thought of Doctor Berkley doing so was terrifying.

"You want the child to read to you, Lady Edith?" the doctor said, glancing at Grace, as Lady Edith tutted.

"Yes, Doctor Berkley. That's what I said, isn't it? So, it's settled, then. I'll send Grace down to you at the appropriate time. And don't worry, I'll be sure to recompense you for your trouble," she said.

The doctor rose to his feet and gave a gracious bow.

"As you wish, Lady Edith," he replied, and with that, he took his leave of them.

Grace was left alone with her patron, and Lady Edith turned to her and sighed.

"My poor child, how I feel for you. You must feel so terribly alone," she said, and Grace nodded.

She still expected her mother to enter the room with a cup of chamomile tea for Lady Edith, or a bottle of tonic or ointment. To think she was gone was the most cruel and terrible of contemplations, one Grace knew she could never fully come to terms with.

"I… I miss her," Grace said, and she began to sob, even as she tried to hold back her tears in the presence of Lady Edith.

"I know you do. We both do. She was a dear companion to me, and you can be, too, Grace," Lady Edith said.

At that moment, a knock came at the door, and Mrs. Parks entered the room, carrying a tray with Lady Edith's dinner on it.

"I'm sorry for the delay, my Lady. It's not been an easy day," she said, glancing at Grace with a withering look.

"Mrs. Parks, take Grace to the kitchens and give her something to eat. No… perhaps not the kitchens, such a terrible scene… she can eat in the dining room," Lady Edith said.

Mrs. Parks looked askance as she set the tray down on Lady Edith's lap.

"The dining room, my Lady?" she replied, and Lady Edith nodded.

"That's what I said, Mrs. Parks, or wherever she prefers. And not what the other servants are eating. Give her something nice to eat. You can come to me any time you wish, Grace, and when you feel ready, go to Doctor Berkley for your lessons," Lady Edith continued.

At these words, Mrs. Parks looked even more horrified, even as Grace nodded and rose to her feet.

"Thank you, Lady Edith," she said, brushing the tears from her eyes.

"But… is she to remain here, my Lady?" Mrs. Parks asked, and Lady Edith nodded.

"That's right, Mrs. Parks. She's to be my ward," Lady Edith replied.

* * *

THE TRAGEDY of the death of Grace's mother was treated with a mixture of sorrow and indifference. Some of the servants expressed their condolences, and Mrs. Lewes brought Grace a cup of tea with three spoonfuls of sugar in it.

"When I saw her lying there... oh, my poor nerves. You poor child, it's too dreadful, too dreadful," she exclaimed, shaking her head.

"Will you eat in the dining room as her Ladyship suggests?" Mrs. Parks asked, the two of them having walked downstairs together in silence.

"Please, I... I don't feel hungry," Grace replied.

She was numb with pain, unable to express the depth of her sorrow. They had walked straight past the place where her mother's body had lay, and Grace could see the image of her mother's face, forever imprinted in her memories, cold and lifeless.

"Her Ladyship was insistent," Mrs. Parks replied.

She herself had expressed no sympathy towards Grace. The matter of the nurse's death was an inconvenience to the running of the household. An incident such as this brought with it the threat of idle gossip, and the matter would soon be the talk of the village.

"Let her do as she pleases, Mrs. Parks. Why don't you go to bed, Grace? You've had a terrible shock. I'll bring you something to eat in the morning," Mrs. Lewes said, looking at Grace sympathetically.

Grace nodded. She did not know how to feel. She wanted only to hide herself away from the world, her heart and mind filled with grief, knowing her mother would not return.

"Very well, Grace. You can go to your room. You've been fortunate to find favour with her Ladyship. If it was up to me..." she said, her words hanging in the air as she shook her head.

Grace nodded. She knew she had been fortunate in Lady Edith's kindness, even as her mother had been the loyalist of companions. Grace had known nothing other than Carshalton House, her whole life confined to the estate and village, and now it seemed she was to remain there, at least for now.

"Are you sure you won't eat something, Grace? Or a hot cup of tea?" Mrs. Lewes whispered, as Grace rose to her feet.

But Grace shook her head. She wanted only to be alone, unable to comprehend the awfulness of what had happened, the sudden change in her life seeming overwhelming.

"I'll be all right," she said, even as her words sounded empty and hollow.

"She's to be apprenticed to the doctor, and taught to read," Mrs. Parks was telling one of the other servants, as Grace made her way up to bed.

The other servant, a man named Roger Parks, tutted, and shook his head.

"And why should she have better opportunities than the rest of us?" he muttered.

Grace ignored them, making her way upstairs to the room she had shared with her mother. The room now belonging to her. It seemed stark, the bed still unmade, her mother's clothes folded neatly on the chair, her few worldly possessions strewn about.

Tears welled up in Grace's eyes, and she sat down heavily on her cot, sobbing, as she lay down and buried her face in the blankets. The kindness of Lady Edith paled into insignificance against the thought of her loss.

Grace would have given anything for her mother's return. She could not bear the thought of life without her, and there, surrounded by her memories, she sobbed the whole night long...

* * *

"Take that, Grace, but don't tell Mrs. Parks," Mrs. Lewes said, handing Grace a slice of bread and dripping and smiling at her.

Grace was due at Doctor Berkley's house that afternoon. It had been a week since her mother had died, and the funeral was to take place the following day. Doctor Berkley had sent word for Grace to come to his cottage in the village that afternoon to begin their reading lessons, even as he had stressed his unsuitability for the task.

"She'd be better off at the village school, Lady Edith," he had said, but Lady Edith had refused to listen, insisting the doctor be the one to teach her.

"And then she'll be there all day long, and I'll have no one to read to me. No, she can learn the things she needs to by reading the books I want to have read to me," Lady Edith had said, and Doctor Berkley had not been able to argue with her reasoning.

In the week since her mother's death, Grace had merely existed. She felt numb, and had shed so many tears, she felt as though she had no more to shed. The curate had come to offer consolation but had also expressed surprise at Lady Edith's decision to allow Grace to remain as her ward.

"Really, Lady Edith, I admire your charity, but for the sake of Grace's future..." he had said, but Lady Edith had refused to hear anymore.

"I don't know why everyone's so against your remaining as my ward. Perhaps the curate's worried I won't leave him any money for his ailing church roof," she had said, smiling maternally at Grace, who knew she had to be grateful.

"But you're not grateful, are you, Grace?" Mrs. Parks had snarled, as she had led Grace back downstairs to the kitchen.

Grace had shaken her head, even as she hardly had the strength to protest. She *was* grateful to Lady Edith for her kindness, but she missed her mother more than she could say and could hardly bear to think of what the future would bring.

"And when Lady Edith dies? What then?" she thought to herself,

as she made her way through the gardens of Carshalton House and into Harebell Woods, where a path wounds its way through the trees towards the village.

The village of Carshalton nestled in a narrow ravine, with a stream flowing through it towards the sea. A long sandy beach stretched out for several miles in one direction, with treacherous cliffs at one end, on which many a passing ship had been dashed and wrecked.

It was rumoured some of these wrecks were deliberate, and hushed whispers occasionally spoke of lights flashed from the cliff tops to lure passing ships to their doom.

"Ah, Grace, come in," Doctor Berkley said when Grace arrived at his red brick cottage on the edge of the village.

It was a pleasant dwelling, covered in ivy and wisteria, and with a thatched roof. The garden was a mass of different vegetables, all growing in neat, regimented lines, the borders filled with flowers, many of which were now bursting into colour as summer approached.

"I'm here at the right time, aren't I, Doctor Berkley?" Grace asked, and the doctor nodded.

"You are, yes. Neither of us had much choice in the matter, did we?" he said, and Grace shook her head.

She did not want to make the doctor angry. She liked him, and her mother had spoken highly of him.

"He's well trained," she had once said–high praise from a woman who considered most physicians to be quacks.

"No, and I'm sorry–" Grace stammered, but Doctor Berkley shook his head and smiled.

"You don't need to be sorry, Grace. I'm glad to help you, though I still don't think I'm the best person to help you. Mr. Dixon at the schoolhouse would've been a better choice. Still, if Lady Edith insists," he said, ushering Grace into his parlour.

It served as a consulting room, with a large desk, and bookcase, and a variety of medical instruments on the shelves. The doctor had placed two chairs opposite one another at a small table, and there was a jug of lemonade and some biscuits set on a tray with glasses.

"It's very kind of you," she said, as he pulled back one of the chairs for her.

"Come now, sit down. We'll see how proficient you are already. Your mother taught you a little, didn't she?" he said, and Grace nodded.

Her mother had taught her to read passages from the Bible. The language was not always easy, and some of the printing in the King James version was difficult to read. Nevertheless, Grace had persevered, and she had gained something of a proficiency, if only in the basics.

Doctor Berkley now took down the same version of the Bible from a shelf, opening it at a random passage and instructing Grace to read.

"Riches profit not in the day of... wrath: but... right...eou... sness deliver...eth from death," Grace read, tracing the words with her fingers.

Doctor Berkley nodded.

"Yes, not bad. Proverbs 11:4. But you'll need a better pace if you're to read to her Ladyship. Trying something longer," he said, turning the pages again.

"In my Father's house are many mansions: if it were not so, I would have told you. I go to prepare a place for you," Grace read.

She knew this verse–it was one of Lady Edith's favourites. Doctor Berkley nodded with satisfaction.

"Better, yes – you'll know the text to be from John 14:2. But we can improve, I'm sure. Now, listen as I read this passage from 1 Corinthians," he said, and turning to the passage, he began to read.

In this way, they passed the following hours, and it seemed Doctor Berkley had consulted various manuals in pedagogy to discover the correct way of teaching Grace to rudiments of reading.

Despite his protests to the contrary, he was an excellent teacher, and Grace found herself better able to follow the text, and by the time they paused for lemonade and biscuits she felt certain it would not be long before her proficiency improved enough for her to read to Lady Edith as her mother had so often done.

"I still need a lot more practice," Grace said when the lesson came to an end.

"A little, yes. But you're much better than I feared you'd be. You're an intelligent girl, Grace. A credit to your mother. I know none of this is easy. My own mother died when I was young. I was raised by my father, but he was a distant figure, and I was on my own a great deal. Books were my solace. Perhaps they can be yours, too. Here, take these volumes of poetry. Practice reading them out loud, and next week, you can recite your favourite one," Doctor Berkley said, rising to his feet, and taking down several small volumes from the shelf.

Grace thanked him. The afternoon had been a distraction, and whilst she had been nervous beforehand, she realized now there was no reason to be so–not anymore. Doctor Berkley was a kind and pleasant man–she could not imagine him raising his voice or growing angry with her, and she was grateful to him for agreeing to do what he had done.

"Thank you, Doctor Berkley," she said, as he showed her out.

"I'll see you next week, or perhaps before, if I'm summoned by her Ladyship," he said.

Grace thanked him again, stepping out in the fragrant air of the garden, where a cuckoo's call was echoing through the trees. She made her way through the village, taking the path through the woods leading to Carshalton House and pausing by a bank of wildflowers, sitting on a mossy stump, and opening one of the volumes of poetry the doctor had given her.

"*Can death be sleep, when life is but a dream, and scenes of bliss pass as a phantom by? The transient pleasures as a vision seem, And yet we think the greatest pain's to die,*" she read, struggling with the words, and more so with the meaning.

It was a poem by John Keats, and Grace could not understand why death should be thought of as a sleep, when she had so willed her mother to awaken from that everlasting slumber.

She sighed, brushing a tear from her eye. The woodland was still, the dappled sunshine coming through the canopy above, and a carpet of bluebells stretching down into the ravine. Grace thought about her mother, longing for just one more moment in her company. She was to be buried in the churchyard the following day, and it felt as though a chapter in Grace's life was closing, a new one yet to be written.

"*I wish it really was a dream,*" she said to herself, brushing away a tear, and praying her mother was still somewhere close, even if out of sight.

READING ALOUD

"*If music be the food of love, play on; Give me excess of it, that, surfeiting, the appetite may sicken, and so die. That strain again! it had a dying fall: O, it came o'er my ear like the sweet sound, That breathes upon a bank of violets, stealing and giving odour! Enough; no more: 'Tis not so sweet now as it was before. O spirit of love! How quick and fresh art thou, That, notwithstanding thy capacity Receiveth as the sea, nought enters there, Of what validity and pitch soe'er, But falls into abatement and low price, Even in a minute: so full of shapes is fancy That it alone is high fantastical,*" Grace read, and when she had finished the speech, Lady Edith raised her hand and smiled.

"I think that's enough for today, Grace. But what beautiful lines to finish with. *Twelfth Night* - it's my favourite play, and you're reading it so well," she said, as Grace closed the volume of Shakespeare she had been reading from.

It was six months after Grace's mother had died. Life at Carshalton House had changed little in that time. Lady Edith spent most of her time in her bedroom, resting on the bed, or lying on the chaise lounge by the window, where she could look out over the gardens.

14

It was winter now, and a fog had enveloped the house for several days. Such fogs were common near the coast, and though Grace was used to them, she still found the atmosphere eery. She had been diligent in her lessons with Doctor Berkley, and her reading was advanced for one of her age and class. She had worked hard and could read almost anything Lady Edith chose for her.

"I like the story," Grace said, and Lady Edith smiled.

"I'm glad. I find Shakespeare so… lyrical. That makes me sound quite naïve, but it's the language, the rhythm of the words. It's hard to describe. But you read it very well–just as your mother used to," she said.

Grace was pleased. She wanted to please Lady Edith, who had been unfailingly kind to her since the death of her mother. Whilst Mrs. Parks continued to treat her with cruel disdain below stairs, Grace was comforted by the kindness of Lady Edith, who always insisted on Grace being given the utmost care and attention.

"Is she really to eat what you're eating, my Lady?" Mrs. Parks had said when Lady Edith had suggested Grace have breakfast with her in the mornings so she could read to her at the beginning of the day.

"Are we really to begrudge the child an egg and a little toast and marmalade?" Lady Edith had replied, and Mrs. Parks had been unable to reason against her.

"It's not right. A servant eating breakfast with her Ladyship," she had muttered, as Grace had followed her down to the kitchen.

"I'm glad you like the way I read it, Lady Edith. Doctor Berkley says there isn't much more to teach me. But I like going to the cottage. We always have lemonade and biscuits after our lesson," Grace said, and Lady Edith smiled.

"I'm glad you enjoy them, and I'm sure the good doctor won't mind your continuing with your lessons. I'll insist on it.

You shouldn't always feel you have to remain in the house. I only wish I could walk in the gardens with you, though perhaps not on a day like this. In the winter, I long for foreign climes— the warmth of the French Riviera," Lady Edith replied, glancing out of the window, where the sea fog was swirling, and only the bare branches of the leafless trees were visible.

Winter's bite was severe that year, and there had already been several spectacular storms, with driving rain and flashes of lightning. Grace had felt afraid, watching from her bedroom window, as rumbles of thunder echoed across the tempestuous seas.

From the upper windows of the house, the sea was visible, rolling in beyond the salt-marshes stretching out from the far end of the garden, where the woods gave way to the sand dunes. It was a wild and lonely place, and the thought of wreckers and smugglers made Grace shudder.

"It's very cold outside, my Lady," Grace said, and Lady Edith nodded.

"Then sit here a little longer. You can share the warmth of my fire. I'm sure Mrs. Parks doesn't allow the servants more than a few lumps of coal for their fire—even though I've told her not to enough times," Lady Edith said, shaking her head.

She was right about Mrs. Parks. The housekeeper kept her own sitting room warmed, but the rest of the servants made do with blankets and finding excuses to enter the warmth of the kitchen whenever they could.

Grace's own bedroom was icy, and she would wrap herself in as many blankets as she could find to go to sleep without shivering.

"It's a lovely fire, my Lady," Grace said, holding out her hands to the glowing coals.

"A cheering sight on a wintery day," Lady Edith replied.

"Would you like me to read to you a little more, my Lady?" Grace asked, but Lady Edith shook her head.

"Not now, child. I find I can only concentrate for a short while. I don't know, I feel... as though I'm slowly slipping away. I lie here day after day, nothing really changes. I find myself with little strength to continue, and little will to want to," she replied.

Grace had never heard Lady Edith speak like this, and she was gripped with a sudden fear as to what would become of her if Lady Edith did "slip away." She knew she had been lucky not to be sent to the orphanage or the poorhouse, of wherever else Mrs. Parks might have placed her had the housekeeper had her own way in the matter. But if Lady Edith died, Grace would have no one to defend her...

"But... you won't... die, will you, Lady Edith?" Grace asked, her lip trembling, tears welling up in her eyes.

Lady Edith looked at her and smiled.

"We all die, Grace. But perhaps my time won't be imminent," Lady Edith replied.

Grace fought back her emotions, even as Lady Edith's words reminded her of her mother. She visited her grave each week, taking whatever flowers she could find in the woodland, and lately, sprigs of holly with their red berries. Sitting by the grave, Grace would talk to her mother, lamenting the sad loss she had endured, and telling her how much she missed her.

"But... what would happen..." Grace stammered, even as she hardly dared speak the words.

Lady Edith shook her head.

"You mustn't worry, child. I'm sorry if I've upset you with my musings on my own mortality. But I'm old, and there's little sense in denying the inevitable. But come now, let's talk of happier things. What play might you read to me next? *A Midsummer Night's Dream,* perhaps?" Lady Edith said, but Grace could not stop thinking about the possibility of Lady Edith's death.

It was morbid, but the thought preoccupied her, and when

later she was sitting by the stove in the kitchen, eating a toasted muffin with butter, the thought was still on her mind.

"Look at her, sitting there, idle," Mrs. Parks said, as she swept into the kitchen, tutting and shaking her head.

"Oh, leave her be, Mrs. Parks. She's not doing anyone any harm," Mrs. Lewes said, rolling her eyes.

The cook had been an ally to Grace. She was always saving titbits for her or passing her a scone or biscuit when the housekeeper was not looking. Mrs. Parks glared at the cook, who was turning the spit over the fire, where several birds were slowly roasting.

"Idle, that's what she is," the housekeeper repeated, and she cuffed Grace across the back of the head, causing her to cry out in pain.

"Please, Mrs. Parks, I've done nothing wrong," Grace exclaimed, rising to her feet and holding up her hands to shield herself from any further blows.

The housekeeper scowled at her.

"And why that miserable face? Don't you enjoy the favour of her Ladyship? If we could all be as idle as you, we'd all of us walk around with smiles on her face," Mrs. Parks exclaimed.

The cook let out a snort, covering her face as she tried hard not to laugh–no one could imagine the housekeeper to be anything but her dour and unpleasant self.

"I... I don't want Lady Edith to die," Grace exclaimed, speaking the words she had feared to utter, even as she had been unable to think of anything else since the morning.

The housekeeper looked at her in surprise, as Mrs. Lewes ceased turning the spit, also looking at Grace with a curious expression on her face.

"Die? Why should she die? What do you know about her Ladyship's condition?" Mrs. Parks exclaimed.

"I... I don't know anything," Grace said, shaking her head.

Mrs. Parks ceased her roughly by the shoulders and shook her.

"You're a nasty little wretch–you know something, don't you? You know she's unwell, worse than we all think. Or perhaps... yes... perhaps you've got it all worked out, wicked child. Your mother... yes, your mother planted the idea in your mind, didn't she? I never trusted the nurse. She always thought of herself above everyone else, and now I know why. Poison, that's what you intend. Telling us you fear her Ladyship dying, and you'll make an act of showing your sorrow, I'm sure. And when we're standing at the graveside, mourning the woman we've served faithfully all these years, we'll discover she's left everything to you," Mrs. Parks exclaimed.

There was a triumphant look on her face as though she truly believed her own incredible story.

Grace was seven years old, and yet the housekeeper was treating her as though she was a master criminal, set on a diabolical plan to poison Lady Edith, who, in her estimation, had been manipulated to the extent of leaving her entire fortune to Grace.

Mrs. Lewes' eyes grew wide with astonishment, even as Grace back away from Mrs. Parks, whose eyes were wide with fury.

"Please, Mrs. Parks, it's nothing like that. I... I'm just worried about her Ladyship. She never leaves her bedroom. She spoke of feeling... tired of life," Grace replied.

The housekeeper raised her hand as though to strike her, but Grace now fled, running up the stairs from the kitchen and not stopping until she had reached the upper floors, breathless, as she hid behind a suit of armour on the long corridor leading to Lady Edith's bedroom.

Mrs. Parks had not followed her, and Grace now began to sob, terrified at the thought of what would happen if Lady Edith *did* die. The housekeeper would waste no time in seeing Grace thrown out of the house.

She actually believed Grace to be capable of murder–a child of seven years old–and now Grace knew her future to be entirely uncertain. Lady Edith was not long for this world, and when the time came, Grace would be the first to know Mrs. Parks' wrath.

* * *

"THE COURSE *of true love never did run smooth; but, either it was different in blood, O cross! Too high to be enthrall'd to low. Or else misgraffed in respect of years, O spite! Too old to be engag'd to young. Or else it stood upon the choice of friends, O hell! To choose love by another's eye,"* Grace read, and Lady Edith smiled, raising her hand–the sign for Grace to stop reading.

"Isn't it wonderful, Grace? And so true, too. The course of true love never did run smooth. Find a person in love who says so? They're a liar," she said, as Grace set aside the volume of Shakespeare, from which she had been reading *A Midsummer Night's Dream.*

She was enjoying the play, with its cast of eccentric characters and its unfortunate comedic twists and turns. Lady Edith had explained a great deal of it to her, and it had proved an ample distraction from her earlier fears. There had been no more talk of death or an unwillingness to live, and it seemed Lady Edith had rallied in her fervours, the lifting of the fog around the house bringing with it a renewed sense of vigour on her part. It was a bright, crisp, cold day, and the sun was shining through the windows, casting its rays through the clouds of dust swirling in the room.

"Were you ever in love, Lady Edith?" Grace asked.

It was a question she would never dared have asked in the past, but Lady Edith treated her as a companion, and had told her she could confide her fear–and her hopes–in her. They had grown close, and Grace felt at ease in the company of the aristocratic lady, whom she was growing increasingly fond of, just as her mother had been before her. Lady Edith gave her a wistful look and smiled.

"I was in love once when I was very young. He was an officer in the militia. My parents disapproved, of course–forbade it. I'd have run away with him. I nearly did–the thought of eloping, oh… it was all so romantic, but… he was sent away. It was my father's influence. The daughter of a duke wasn't to be permitted to marryy a mere officer in the militia. It was all so sad. I wept for a month, and to spite my parents, I refused to love again. That much, I had power over. I was true to my word. I told my parents I wouldn't marry, and I didn't," Lady Edith said.

Grace was surprised at her openness. She had never heard Lady Edith speak in such candid terms. She had always seemed a distant figure, despite their growing intimacy. But these words–words about falling in love–made her appear suddenly vulnerable.

"Are you… happy, Lady Edith?" Grace asked, for she could not imagine how life would be if she never fell in love.

Lady Edith thought for a moment and shook her head.

"It's too late to change it now. But… I've been happy, yes. Falling in love isn't the only path to happiness, of course. I've lived a good life, and I've known companionship, and the pleasures of friendship, too," she replied.

"My mother never spoke about love. She rarely spoke about my father, either," Grace replied.

Grace did not know her father. Her mother had told her only vague stories from her past. She knew nothing of how they had met, how they had come to Norfolk, or what had really happened to him. With her mother's death, such knowledge was lost, and Grace doubted she would ever know the truth about her father's past.

She knew little of her mother, either. It was as though her mother's life was limited to Carshalton House, and her time in service to Lady Edith as her nurse. Grace's mother had been twenty-eight years old when she had died, and of those twenty-eight years, Grace knew hardly anything.

"Oh, but she loved you, Grace. Whatever might be said, she loved you," Lady Edith replied.

Grace felt surprised to hear these words. She did not understand what Lady Edith meant by them, nor what might be said against the fact of her mother's love for her.

"She always told me she loved me, my Lady," Grace replied.

"Your mother was a good woman, Grace. She did everything she could for you. You were... her most precious treasure," Lady Edith said.

Grace smiled. She was able to think of her mother without tears welling up in her eyes. It was not easy, but with the passing of time, the sorrow of her loss was lessening, replaced with the comforting memories of what had been. Her mother *had* loved her, and Grace clung to that knowledge in hope of a better future, even as she still feared Lady Edith's loss.

"What more can you tell me about her, Lady Edith?" Grace asked, and Lady Edith smiled.

"She was my nurse for nine years. Your father... worked away. I rarely saw him. But when you arrived, your mother was so happy. His death broke her heart–as well it would. But she was possessed of a great inner strength. But I fear the burden of her sorrows was what killed her. She worried about so many things. I fear it was an ailment of the mind. But I shouldn't be saying these things to you. You want to remember her as she was. Your mother was a good and kind woman, and never let anyone tell you differently," Lady Edith replied.

Again, Grace was confused, but she did not press Lady Edith

for further details, as she took up the volume of Shakespeare to read again.

"*I know a bank where the wild thyme blows, where oxlips and the nodding violet grows, Quite over-canopied with luscious woodbine, With sweet musk-roses and with eglantine,*" she read, opening the volume at a different page, and as she did so, she thought of her mother, and the many happy walks they had taken together in the woodland around the house.

"*And that's how I'll remember her,*" Grace told herself, even as she wondered why anyone would speak differently of her mother, who had surely been the kindest, gentlest creature Grace had ever known.

THE INHERITANCE

"Are you taking this tonic, my Lady?" Doctor Berkley asked, looking sceptically at the half-empty bottle on the bedside table.

Lady Edith nodded.

"I mightn't have a nurse, Doctor Berkley, but I still follow your orders, don't worry," she said, glancing at Grace, who knew Lady Edith regularly poured quantities of the foul-smelling liquid out of the window.

The doctor nodded, closing his medical bag, and rising from the chair by the bedside.

"I'm worried about your heart rate, Lady Edith. It seems somewhat erratic when I listen to it. I want you to assure me as to how you feel? Are you too hot? Too cold? Do you shiver?" he asked.

"Doctor Berkley, I feel quite well, though not what I once was, of course. A clock needs winding if it's to keep time, and I feel my own clockwork slowing. Does that make sense?" she asked, and the doctor nodded.

"It does, my Lady. We all face slowing down as the years go by. Tonics and medicines can be a help, of course. But there's no

Holy Grail, no true elixir of life. You must rest," he said, nodding to Lady Edith, who waved her hand dismissively.

"It's always the same, Doctor Berkley. More rest, but I've nothing to rest from. I do nothing but rest. Am I to rest from rest?" she asked.

The doctor did not answer that question, and having bid Grace goodbye, he left the room.

"Shall I read to you, my Lady?" Grace asked, but Lady Edith shook her head.

"No... thank you, Grace. I'd like to be alone, I think. I can't stand those foul-smelling tonics he prescribes–even if they're meant to do me good. But I can't go on pretending I'll last forever," Lady Edith replied.

It made Grace sorrowful to think it, and she hurried out of the room, making her way downstairs to the kitchens. As she came to the landing above the scullery, she could hear voices below.

The scullery was separate from the kitchen, and usually reserved for the pot-washers and maids of all work to wash the dirty dishes and pans. But to Grace's surprise, it was the hushed tones of Mrs. Parks, talking to a man whose voice Grace recognised as that of Dolby Cleverley, an unpleasant man who worked in the gardens, and whom Grace always tried to avoid.

"I'm telling you, she's not long for this world. We've got to act now," Mrs. Parks was saying.

"And you really think she's going to leave the jewellery to the girl?" Dolby replied.

Grace froze, shrinking back from the balustrade, terrified at what she was hearing.

"I don't know–but she's going to leave her something. But she's always there in her bedroom. I don't know... a sleeping draught, perhaps," Mrs. Parks replied.

Grace's eyes grew wide with horror. They were plotting to rob Lady Edith, who had thousands of pounds' worth of jewellery in her bedroom. She had once shown it to Grace–diamond tiaras, sapphire brooches, pearl earrings, a ruby necklace inlaid with gold and silver.

"Yes, something slipped into her tea. You'd have to be the one to do it, though, Mrs. Parks. If she awoke and found you there, you'd have a reason for being so. If I was the one..." Dolby said, his words trailing off.

"And what would I owe you, Dolby? If I do it all myself, what's your part?" Mrs. Parks replied.

"Keeping my mouth shut, Mrs. Parks. Don't forget what I know. All the things you slip into your pockets. You've made yourself quite a tidy sum these years gone by, haven't you?" he said.

Grace remembered her mother saying something about the housekeeper's light hands, and whilst she would gladly have fled in fear, she felt compelled to listen further as the details of this wicked plan were hatched.

"And I could tell a few tales about you, Dolby–and don't forget it. Very well, you bring me something to help her sleep. I'll take the jewels. She'll think she's mislaid them. She's too weak and feeble for anything else. We'll hide the jewellery, and when it comes to the reading of the will, no one will know the difference," she said, and Dolby laughed.

"You're a wicked woman, Mrs. Parks–and you're fortunate I'm a wicked man. I'll get you what you need, you do the deed, and we'll keep one another's secret," he said.

At these words, the housekeeper and the gardener left the scullery, and Grace turned and hurried back up the stairs towards the landing, terrified at what she had just heard. She was about to go straight to Lady Edith and tell her everything she had heard, fearful the wicked plan would be enacted at once. But as she came to the door of Lady Edith's bedroom, she paused, thinking twice before knocking.

"It would terrify her, and what could she do? She's powerless

against them," Grace said to herself, and she shook her head, knowing she would need the help of someone else if she was to save Lady Edith from such a terrible fate.

None of the other servants could be trusted—there was no telling which of them knew of the plot, and which of them might also be involved. Even Mrs. Lewes—whom Grace knew had no love for Mrs. Parks—could not be trusted to keep such a terrible secret.

There was only one person whom Grace could trust, and that was Doctor Berkley. Turning away from Lady Edith's bedroom door, Grace hurried back along the corridor, taking the back stairs and letting herself out of a side door into the garden. There was no time to lose—Lady Edith's life depended on it.

* * *

"THEY'RE GOING TO DO WHAT?" Doctor Berkley exclaimed, his eyes wide with horror and astonishment as Grace breathlessly told him what she had overheard.

She had run all the way to the doctor's house, arriving out of breath and banging hard at the door.

"They're going to give her a sleeping draught and rob her. Even if she notices the jewels are gone, they believe she'll be dead before anyone realises. They think she's going to leave them to me," Grace said, repeating the explanation she had already given.

Doctor Berkley shook his head.

"What wickedness this is. I don't doubt they believe she's not long for this world. I fear it myself, but... to hasten her to the grave... if they administer too strong a draught, she may never awaken from it. They're proposing murder," he exclaimed, shuddering as he spoke the words.

"That's why I had to tell you. I didn't know what else to do," Grace replied.

Doctor Berkley placed his hand on her shoulder.

"You've done the right thing, Grace. I know it must've terrified you to hear them speak such wicked words, but... we can prevent it," he said, furrowing his brow, as though desperately thinking how to do so.

"But what if they do it tonight?" Grace exclaimed.

"Ah, now, that we *can* prevent. A sleeping draught isn't an easy thing to confect, or get hold of. I know of only one place in the village," he said, turning towards his own cabinet of medicine with a knowing look, tapping his nose and smiling.

"What if Dolby tries to rob you, Doctor Berkley?" Grace exclaimed, for she felt certain the gardener would go to any lengths to secure that which was needed to enact their wicked plan.

"I'll take the sleeping drafts with me, and I'll go at once to Carshalton House and speak with Lady Edith. She asked me about changing her will only recently. She *does* want to favour you, but I fear she'd only make her enemies angrier and place you in danger after her death. No, I've got a better idea," the doctor said, as Grace stared at him in astonishment.

She had not realised Lady Edith planned to favour her in her will, and she had certainly done nothing to encourage it. Grace was only a child, and innocent of such worldly thoughts and ambitions.

Lady Edith had asked her to read to her, to learn from Doctor Berkley, and keep her company in these, her final days. Grace had done so, knowing it was what her mother would have wanted her to do, as she herself had done.

"But please, don't tell her what you know. It would terrify her," Grace said, fearful of Lady Edith discovering the truth about the plot to steal her jewellery.

"No, no, we'll keep it a secret, Grace. I'll suggest Lady Edith would help you better by selling the jewels and using the money to establish a trust fund in your name. This could provide for you when reach a suitable age, eighteen, perhaps. It would be up to her Ladyship's heir to administer the fund, but they'd be bound by law to honour it, and Mrs. Parks and her compatriots would be prevented from taking the jewellery for themselves. I can offer to make the arrangements, and suggest the jewellery be hidden somewhere other than Lady Edith's bedroom," Doctor Berkley replied.

Grace nodded. It was a bold plan, even as she remained astonished to think Lady Edit meant to favour her in such a way. She felt entirely unworthy of such a gift and humbled to think her mother had been the one to pave the way for such generosity.

"Do you think we can stop them, Doctor Berkley?" she asked, and the doctor nodded.

"We can certainly foil their plans. But if I know Mrs. Parks, she'll have other nefarious ideas as to how she might defraud her Ladyship. I've been anxious about the possibility for some time. I don't trust her—or any of the servants. She's the one who runs the household, not Lady Edith. It's she who has the power," Doctor Berkley said, shaking his head.

Having removed the sleeping draught from his medicine cabinet, Doctor Berkley told Grace to accompany him back to Carshalton House. The weather was closing in, and the bright wintery day of the morning was being swiftly replaced by dark clouds rolling in from the sea. There was a squall in the air, and by the time they reached the house, it was beginning to rain heavily.

"We can go in through the side door," Grace said, hoping to avoid Mrs. Parks or any of the other servants—especially Dolby.

But as they made their way along the terrace, Grace spotted the gardener watching them.

"Good day, Doctor Berkley. It's turning nasty. You've arrived just in time," the gardener said, and Doctor Berkley nodded.

"Yes, I fear I'll have to shelter here for some time after my consultation with her Ladyship. I doubt I'll be home before it gets dark," the doctor replied as Grace opened the side door for them, and they hurried inside.

"He'll know you're out," Grace said, looking up at Doctor Berkley in confusion.

But the doctor smiled.

"Precisely. And when he breaks into my house, he'll find no sleeping draught in the medicine cabinet," he replied, smiling, and winking at Grace as he spoke.

They made their way upstairs, through the maze of corridors and staircases, arriving at Lady Edith's door, just as Mrs. Parks was taking in a tray. Grace's eyes grew wide with horror— on the tray, steaming with the scent of chamomile, was a cup and saucer.

"Doctor Berkley, whatever brings you here?" Mrs. Parks said, glancing at Grace, her lips pursed and angry.

"I'm the village doctor, Mrs. Parks—Lady Edith is one of my patients. I visit all my patients regularly, and not always with an appointment," Doctor Berkley replied.

The housekeeper forced a smile on her face.

"I was just taking her Ladyship some tea—chamomile tea, so soothing, don't you think?" she said.

"I prefer cocoa, myself. I'll take it to her. I was just going in," Doctor Berkley replied, and handing Grace his medical bag, he insisted on taking the tray from the housekeeper, who had no grounds to refuse him.

Lady Edith, too, was surprised to see the doctor entering the room. He did not make a habit of arriving unannounced, but Grace was relieved to know she had convinced him of the seriousness of Mrs. Parks' wicked intentions.

The chamomile tea was surely a precursor to something far

worse, a practice run for the administration of the poison, and it made Grace shudder to think how easily harm could come to the invalided aristocrat, who would surely think nothing of a cup of tea brought under the auspices of kindness.

"Oh, Doctor Berkley, Grace–how nice to see you both. Mrs. Parks was just bringing me, oh… it's there," Lady Edith said, as she sat up in bed.

To Grace's surprise, Doctor Berkley suddenly tripped on the edge of the Persian rug by the hearth, sending the tray–and the cup of chamomile tea–crashing to the ground. He hurried to apologise, and Grace noticed he took up a piece of the cup–stained with tea leaves–and slipped it into his pocket.

"My Lady, I can only apologise," he exclaimed, scrambling to his feet, and dusting himself down.

Lady Edith smiled and waved her hand dismissively.

"Oh, there's no harm done. I don't really care for chamomile tea, though I wouldn't dare say so to Mrs. Parks. It was kind of her to bring it. But this is quite the unexpected visit," she said, glancing affectionately at Grace, who hurried to her side.

"Are you feeling quite well, Lady Edith?" she asked, for they could not dismiss the possibility the poison had been administered by some other means than the chamomile tea now soaking into the Persian rug, its earthy scent hanging in the air.

Lady Edith nodded.

"Oh, yes, quite well, thank you, Grace. I was going to ask for you later–you could read to me. But something other than Shakespeare. The Bible, perhaps," she said, and Grace nodded.

She was relieved to find Lady Edith well, but it would surely be only a matter of time before Mrs. Parks–or one of the other servants–made a second attempt. Doctor Berkley looked concerned.

"Lady Edith, have you noticed anything… untoward lately?" he asked.

Lady Edith looked surprised.

"I don't know what you mean, doctor?" she asked.

"About your health, I mean? Do you feel it's deteriorating at all?" he asked.

Lady Edith thought for a moment and shook her head.

"I've had the occasional headache, but nothing more than that, no. If anything, I feel better than before," she replied.

"That's very good. I'm glad to hear it. I wanted to speak to you about... well, the matter we spoke of just the other day. The changing of your will," he said, and Lady Edith smiled.

"Yes, I was going to mention it to Grace, though I know she's too young to understand fully," she replied, glancing at Grace, who understood better than her benefactor believed.

She knew Lady Edith was dying. She had been in a steady state of decline for many years, even as Grace's mother had done all she could to care for her. Lady Edith had often told Grace's mother she would take care of her and Grace in her will, and Grace's mother had smiled and nodded, assuring Lady Edith there were still many years before such thoughts were necessary. But the time had come, and with Grace's mother dead, Lady Edith's will would favour Grace herself.

"I'm sure she can understand well enough. But I have a suggestion, my Lady. Why not sell some of your jewels now and establish a fund for Grace? The bulk of your estate goes to your distant cousin, but unless he marries, your jewels will mean nothing to him. If Grace was to inherit them, there's little she could do but sell them herself, and that might prove difficult for one so young and easily manipulated," Doctor Berkley said.

Lady Edith thought for a moment, nodding as she glanced at Grace, who was standing quietly by the bedside.

"Yes, an excellent suggestion, Doctor Berkley. I hadn't thought of that. You're right, a fund would serve her better. My jewels lie idly on the dressing table, but they could be made to work harder, couldn't they? It's not as though I'll ever wear them again," Lady Edith replied, sighing, and closing her eyes.

Grace felt sorry for her. She was coming to the end of her life, and when she died, Grace knew there would be many changes at Carshalton House–especially for her.

She would be sent away, and she doubted Lady Edith's generosity would go uncontested. The contents of the will would be challenged, and even if the jewellery could be saved for the moment, there was no doubt in Grace's mind as to her future fate. She would be sent away, and Mrs. Parks and the other servants would get what they wanted, one way or another.

"And they'd be safer, too, my Lady," Doctor Berkley replied.

Lady Edith sighed and nodded.

"I've thought the same, Doctor Berkley. We live in a lonely position, far from law and order. Things happen here, and… well, I shouldn't say it, should I," she said, opening her eyes for a moment and glancing towards the door.

Doctor Berkley cleared his throat.

"Perhaps they'd be better kept under lock and key. I could arrange it for you," he said, and Lady Edith nodded.

"I've a place of my own to put them, Doctor Berkley. Fear not, I know danger haunts me," she said, as footsteps approached the door.

A sharp knock was followed by the entrance of the house-keeper, who looked surprised to find the china cup shattered, and the scent of the chamomile tea lingering in the air.

"My Lady, I thought…" she began, but Lady Edith waved her hand dismissively.

"I didn't really want it, anyway, Mrs. Parks. I want to get up. I've got some things to do," she said, glancing at the jewellery on her dressing table.

The housekeeper looked angry, but she said nothing, nodding, before helping Lady Edith out of bed.

"I'll take my leave, my Lady," Doctor Berkley said, but Lady Edith shook her head.

"No, Doctor Berkley, wait a moment. I want to give you the key to my safe. I'll lock the jewels there until you can make the necessary arrangements. But leaving the key here would be folly, I think, don't you?" she said.

Grace realised what Lady Edith was doing and could only presume she already suspected the housekeeper of foul play. Mrs. Parks looked incensed, but there was nothing she could say, and the jewels were locked in a small safe in the corner of the room, before Lady Edith handed the key to Doctor Berkley for safe keeping.

"I'll take good care of it, I promise," the doctor said, before taking his leave.

Mrs. Parks, too, made her excuses–no doubt intending to tell the other servants of this inconvenient development immediately–and Grace was left alone with Lady Edith.

"I do mean for you to be taken care of, Grace. I promise you. Though I can't assure you, other powers won't work against my plans," she said.

Grace nodded. She did not want anything from Lady Edith, only for her to remain the one bright light in her otherwise unhappy existence.

"I promise I'll do my best for you, Lady Edith," Grace said, and Lady Edith smiled.

"You're certainly your mother's child, Grace. You mightn't understand that now, but you will. One day, you will," she replied, as Grace took up the Bible next to the bed and opened it to read.

AN UNEXPECTED LEGACY

"Nasty child. Nasty, wicked child," Mrs. Parks snarled, as Grace entered the kitchen.

It was nothing new. Ever since the incident with the chamomile tea–which Doctor Berkley suspected contained a small dose of arsenic–Mrs. Parks had treated Grace with ever greater contempt. Grace had said nothing.

She had not accused Mrs. Parks of treachery, nor did the housekeeper have any proof she knew anything of the wicked plan to steal Lady Edith's jewels. But with the tiaras, necklaces, rings, and earrings now locked safely in the safe, and Doctor Berkley holding the key, the chance of stealing them before Lady Edith could change her will was gone. This had been swiftly accomplished, and provision had been made for Grace–a fund to pay for education and her future.

"I want you to be looked after, Grace," Lady Edith had promised, and it seemed the matter was settled–much to the anger of Mrs. Parks and the other servants.

"Leave her be, Mrs. Parks," Mrs. Lewes said, glancing at Edith, who was warming her hands on the fire.

It was late February, and winter was far from in abeyance.

Mrs. Lewes had given her a crumpet for breakfast, hot and buttered, fresh from the griddle, and now she looked up at Mrs. Parks, who had come to prepare Lady Edith's breakfast tray, it being the maid's morning off.

"I haven't done anything, Mrs. Parks. I'm just sitting here by the fire," Grace said, and the housekeeper raised her hand angrily.

"Your being here–that's what you've done. You've turned her against us all. You and that doctor," she snarled, banging the tray down on the kitchen table as Mrs. Lewes brought the muffin warmer and a pot of jam with a silver spoon.

"She hasn't got anywhere else to go, Mrs. Parks. And it's her Ladyship's decision," the cook said.

Mrs. Lewes was Grace's only friend below stairs. The other servants treated her with only thinly veiled disdain, and Mrs. Parks now grimaced.

"Yes, but perhaps her Ladyship isn't right in her decision," she said, taking up the tray and marching out of the kitchen.

Mrs. Lewes shook her head and sighed.

"I don't know… what a strange place this is," she said.

"How long have you been here, Mrs. Lewes?" Grace asked, and the cook smiled.

"Too long. I remember your mother arriving, and… well, that was a long time ago," she said.

Grace was about to question her further when a sudden scream echoed from above stairs, and the voice of Mrs. Parks called out from the upper landing.

"She's dead!" she cried, and Grace's eyes grew wide with horror.

The other servants–who had been enjoying their hot buttered crumpets at the kitchen table–leaped to their feet, running up the stairs at the housekeeper's summons. Grace followed, her heart beating fast, tears welling up in her eyes.

She had said goodnight to Lady Edith the evening before,

having read the first scenes of *Anthony and Cleopatra* to her. Lady Edith had seemed in good spirits and had promised to try to get up the following day to walk in the gardens, even as she had feared her strength would fail her.

"How fortunate I am to have you, Grace. You've become like a granddaughter to me," she had said, placing her hand to Grace's cheek and smiling.

There had been no indication she was close to death, and Grace had promised to return after breakfast the following day. But now she came to the landing, finding Mrs. Park standing at the door to Lady's Edith's bedroom, her face white, and her eyes wide with horror.

"I'll go in," Dolby, the gardener, said, pushing past the others and entering Lady Edith's bedroom.

It would be unthinkable for him to have done so if she was alive. But now the other servants crowded around the doorway, peering cautiously inside. Grace stood amongst them, craning her neck, fearful of what she would see.

Lady Edith was lying half on, half off the bed, as though she had collapsed trying to get up. Her face was pale, her eyes wide and blankly staring.

"I was just bringing the tray in," Mrs. Parks said, the remains of Lady Edith's breakfast lying strewn across the Persian rug.

Dolby looked up from the bedside and nodded.

"She's dead–I'd say she's been dead all night. Who was the last one to see her alive?" he asked, and Mrs. Parks turned to Grace.

"She was. Her Ladyship insisted on being read to last thing at night. She didn't want her chamomile tea–she said it was tasting bitter lately," she said, as the other servants looked accusingly at Grace.

"I... I said goodnight to her after I'd finished reading to her. But she was fine then," Grace stammered, as shocked as anyone to find Lady Edith dead.

Mrs. Parks shook her head.

"Fetch Doctor Berkley, though it'll do no good. I'll send for her solicitor," she said, as though the matter of Lady Edith's death was to be treated as a formality, rather than a tragedy.

Lady Edith was laid on the bed and covered with a blanket and two shillings placed over her eyes. Grace stood watching, fighting back the tears.

She had remained at Carshalton House purely on the kindness of her benefactor, and whilst provision had been made for her, it would be necessary for the heir to administer Lady Edith's kindness. As she made her way downstairs, hoping it would not be long before Doctor Berkley arrived, Mrs. Parks caught her roughly by the shoulder.

"Please..." Grace stammered, shrinking back in fear, as the housekeeper brought her face down close to hers.

"I'm watching you, Grace. I know what you've done. I know she's changed her will. Don't think I'll forget it," the housekeeper snarled, her grip on Grace's arm growing tighter.

"But I don't care about all that. I just want her back. She was like a mother to me, a grandmother," Grace stammered, as the housekeeper's eyes narrowed.

"Yes... and you used that to your advantage, didn't you? I know what you've done. You and the doctor. Well, you'll not be here for much longer. When Captain Dickinson arrives, you'll be gone," she said, pushing Grace aside and striding off along the corridor, her keys jangling at her side.

Grace breathed a deep sigh, leaning against the wall of the corridor, hardly able to comprehend the awfulness of what had happened, and how her life had now changed. Captain Stephen Dickinson was a distant relative of Lady Edith.

He had visited Carshalton House a number of times, but had never spoken to Grace, or even deigned to acknowledge her. He was a stern and foreboding man, and Grace did not think he would be in the least sympathetic to her plight.

"Which means I'll have to leave," Grace told herself, even as she did not know where she would go or what she would do...

* * *

"I BELIEVE she died of natural causes," Doctor Berkley said, looking at Grace with a sympathetic expression.

Grace breathed a sigh of relief.

"She wasn't poisoned?" she asked, and the doctor shook his head.

"I think our warning was enough to prevent their plan from taking root. The jewels were under lock and key, her will was changed–she favoured you–and when the solicitor arrives from London, we'll know the details of what she decided," Doctor Berkley replied.

It was three days after Lady Edith's death, and with nothing to do around the house–except be reminded of the terrible circumstances in which she now found herself–Grace had come to the physician's cottage, where a roaring fire burned in the hearth, and the two of them were eating crumpets secretly provided by Mrs. Lewes.

"I'm glad to hear it, though it makes little difference. I miss her terribly," Grace said, sighing as the doctor looked at her sympathetically.

"She was good to you, Grace, and you were good to her. I'm sure your mother would be proud of you for helping her as you did. For a child to learn to read as you've done... it's quite remarkable," he said, and Grace smiled.

"I liked reading to her. We read so many of Shake-speare's plays, and so much of the Bible, too," she said, thinking back to the many hours she had spent at Lady Edith's bedside.

They had been happy times, and Lady Edith had done so much to help her in the aftermath of her mother's death.

"I'm sure she appreciated it. But… things won't be the same now, will they?" he said.

Grace shook her head. Mrs. Parks was making daily threats as to her future.

"It'll not be long before you're gone, Grace," she would say with a smirk.

"I know they won't. But Lady Edith promised to take care of me. It's the funeral tomorrow, and Captain Dickinson's coming from London with the solicitor for the reading of the will," Grace replied.

She had overheard Mrs. Parks telling one of the housemaids to have the captain's chambers prepared, and the funeral was to take place in the parish church, presided over by the curate, who had always thought Grace should be sent away.

"I'll be there, of course. But Grace… you've got to be prepared for the worst. I doubt Captain Dickinson will let you stay at Carshalton House. He's hardly going to want a ward to read to him, and whilst we saved Lady Edith's jewels from the hands of Mrs. Parks, I doubt her promises to you will go uncontested," Doctor Berkley said.

Grace nodded. She knew there were challenges ahead. Captain Dickinson was spoken of in hushed tones by the other servants, and Grace recalled Lady Edith despairing of him as her heir.

"He never comes to see me, and I doubt he'll shed a single tear when I'm gone," she had once said.

"Then I don't know what I'll do," Grace replied.

She was only seven years old, and yet she had known such sorrow in her short life, losing the only people who had ever truly loved her. Doctor Berkley looked at her with a sympathetic gaze.

"I'm sure it'll be all right, Grace. Let's see what tomorrow brings," he replied, offering her another crumpet.

* * *

"FORASMUCH as it hath pleased Almighty God of his great mercy to take unto himself the soul of our dear sister here departed: we therefore commit her body to the ground; earth to earth, ashes to ashes, dust to dust; in sure and certain hope of the Resurrection to eternal life, through our Lord Jesus Christ; who shall change our vile body, that it may be like unto his glorious body, according to the mighty working, whereby he is able to subdue all things to himself," the curate said, as several of the mourners threw handfuls of dirt into the grave.

The day was bitterly cold, and dark clouds hung menacingly above. The wind was blowing, sweeping through the bare branches of the trees around the churchyard, where most of the village had gathered to hear Lady Edith's funeral rites. Grace was standing next to Doctor Berkley, watching as Mrs. Parks stepped forward, a black veil over her face and tears running down her cheeks.

"Goodbye, my Lady," she said, with an almost theatrical turn in her voice, casting her handful of dirt into the grave and shaking her head.

Grace knew this was all for show. The housekeeper had said as much at breakfast that morning, boasting of her position in Captain Dickinson's new household. She would remain the housekeeper and had every intention of seeing Grace thrown out as soon as the heir took possession of his rights. The captain himself stood at the head of the grave. He was a tall man, with a red face and greying hair. He wore a long overcoat and black mourning dress, and stood stiffly to attention, watching as the curate pronounced the final prayers and blessing.

"A sad day," Doctor Berkley said, shaking his head, as the mourners now dispersed.

Standing at the far end of the churchyard by the lychgate, was a man dressed in tweeds, though with the appearance of one who finds himself uncomfortable in the countryside, his shoes spattered with mud, and a briefcase tucked under his arm. As Grace and Doctor Berkley approached, he stepped forward, blocking their path.

"You must be Grace," he said, and Grace nodded, though she did not know who the man was.

"I'm Grace, yes," she said, as the man held out his hand.

"I'm Mr. Fletcher, Horace Fletcher–Lady Edith's solicitor," he replied.

But before he could say anything further, a brusque voice behind had interrupted.

"Mr. Fletcher, let's get this over with, but not out here. I've stood for long enough in the bleakness of this churchyard. We'll return to Carshalton House. You'd better come, too, Doctor Berkley–you were the architect of this, after all," and turning, Grace found Captain Dickinson standing behind them, accompanied by Mrs. Parks.

Doctor Berkley stepped forward, holding out his hand to Captain Dickinson, who looked at him disdainfully.

"Captain Dickinson, we've not had the pleasure," he began, but the captain dismissed him with a wave of his hand.

"It's hardly a pleasure, Doctor Berkley, not when I discover you've interfered in my cousin's will. No doubt to your own advantage. But I won't discuss it here," he said, beckoning for them all to follow him.

The captain returned to Carshalton House in a carriage with Mrs. Parks and the solicitor. Grace and Doctor Berkley walked. The wind was bitter, and the woodland, with its bare trees, offered little protection from the weather.

"It's what I feared–a contesting of the will. I knew he would, but it's still a bitter blow. Lady Edith wanted you to be provided for. It wasn't a case of interfering, and it's not as though she left you the house. She sold certain pieces of jewellery to provide a fund for your future. But it just proves what he's like. Come now, Grace, we must be strong," Doctor Berkley said as they made their way through the gardens.

It was Mrs. Parks who let them in, casting a disdainful look at them both, before leading them in silence to the drawing room.

Captain Dickinson was sitting by the fire, and he did not rise as they entered the room, nor invite them to sit. Mr. Fletcher, who looked thoroughly uncomfortable, was sitting at a table next to one of the many aspidistra plants Lady Edith had culti-vated around the house, shuffling papers from his briefcase.

"Will you have some tea, sir?" Mrs. Parks asked, addressing the captain, rather than anyone else.

"No, I want this over with quickly. Get on with it, Fletcher. Read the will," he said, pointing to the solicitor, who cleared his throat.

Captain Dickinson had not even acknowledged the presence of Grace and Doctor Berkley, and was now staring straight ahead, his face set in a thunderous expression of anger.

"Well, it's quite simple. Lady Edith's will consists of her legacy to you, Captain Dickinson, as her only male heir. You inherit Carshalton House, the estate, and the income rights. There's a title, too—that of the Lord Carshalton, now revived on Lady Edith's death. The contents of the house are yours, too. But some further clauses remain," the solicitor said, shuffling his papers once again.

"Yes, and what are these clauses?" Captain Dickinson replied, glancing at Mrs. Parks, who had remained standing by the door.

Grace knew the housekeeper was expecting her share. She had worked at Carshalton House for many years and had always spoken of her expectations below stairs.

"I know what's coming my way. Her Ladyship won't forget me," she had said, whilst also bad-mouthing her employer at every turn.

"Lady Edith recently instructed me in the sale of a number

pieces of jewellery, totalling several thousand pounds. The funds raised are now in trust, and the income intended to provide for Grace Carruthers, the child named as Lady Edith's ward. Now, the matter requires you, as the heir, to administer the-" Mr. Fletcher said, but he had not finished speaking before Captain Dickinson had leaped angrily from his chair and was pointing his finger at Grace.

"And what right does she have to this? Am I to be made a fool of? Who is she? My cousin's ward. My cousin's downfall, more like. I won't hear of it. If I'm to administer the fund, she gets nothing. I know the sort–she's ingratiated herself, spurned on by the doctor, no doubt. And what share do you take, Doctor Berkley?" Captain Dickinson exclaimed.

The veins on his forehead were standing out, and he was shaking with anger. Grace shrank back in fear, and Doctor Berkley stepped forward.

"Please, Captain Dickinson, you're quite mistaken. Grace is only a child. Her mother was Lady Edith's nurse, and your cousin only wanted to make provision for her. It's hardly comparable to your own inheritance," he said, but Captain Dickinson now seized him by the scruff of the collar.

"You made her change her will. The money was meant for her loyal servants. Nurses are the worst. They ingratiate themselves, then administer the poison. Is that what you did? Mrs. Parks told me everything," Captain Dickinson said, pushing Doctor Berkley angrily away as Mr. Fletcher rose to his feet.

"I'm sure these matters can be agreed on in an amicable way," he said, but Captain Dickinson turned to him, red face and in a terrible rage.

"And you're just as bad for allowing it. But let me tell you this–there won't be any money for the girl. She gets nothing. Do you hear me? Nothing. And I want her out of here. She's not to remain under this roof for a moment longer," he snarled, turning to Grace, and pointing to the drawing-room door.

Mrs. Parks was smirking, and she opened the door, watching as Doctor Berkley took Grace by the hand.

"She's only a child, Captain Dickinson. You're shouting at a child. She's done nothing wrong and was a friend to Lady Edith when no one else was. Your cousin wanted her to have the money–a small gesture of kindness for a child who's lost everything, and now even more so thanks to your cruelty," he said.

"Get out!" Captain Dickinson cried, his eyes wide with anger, and Doctor Berkley led Grace to the door, where Mrs. Parks remained smirking.

"She can collect her things later on from the kitchen door," the housekeeper said.

Doctor Berkley made no reply, and he and Grace left the drawing room, the door of which was now closed behind them. In the hallway, Grace began to sob. She had lost everything and was now all alone in the world.

"It's all right, don't cry, Grace. I'm sorry for the way he behaved. It could all have been so much easier," Doctor Berkley replied, shaking his head.

"But what am I to do?" Grace asked, for she had nowhere to go and no sense of what she would do next.

Lady Edith had provided for her, but Captain Dickinson now refused to allow the money to be hers. Grace felt powerless against such wickedness, and tears rolled down her cheeks.

"Well... for now, you'll have to come with me," Doctor Berkley said, still holding Grace's hand in his.

She looked up at him in surprise. Doctor Berkley had taught her to read. He had been kind to her, and the two of them had become friends. But as for going to live with him...

"But I can't ask that of you, can I? It's not fair. You've already done so much for me," Grace said, but Doctor Berkley shook his head.

"It was Lady Edith who asked me to take you in. She feared her cousin wouldn't follow her instructions and gave me a sum of money before she died. It's not a lot–she hoped her will would be carried out–but it's enough. I won't see you go to an orphanage or a poorhouse, Grace. We'll manage, though I can't promise I'll be much of a companion. My work absorbs me, and I'm not particularly domesticated, but-" he began, even as Grace flung her arms around him in gratitude.

"Oh, thank you, Doctor Berkley. I thought… I feared… oh, but it doesn't matter now," she said, just as the drawing-room door opened and Mrs. Parks appeared, glaring at Grace and Doctor Berkley as she passed.

"You'd better get going. It's a long walk to the orphanage from here," she said, with a gleeful note in her voice, even as she herself had not benefitted one bit from Lady Edith's will, as much as she had expected to do so.

"She's not going to the orphanage, Mrs. Parks. She's coming with me. We'll return for her things tomorrow. Good day to you," Doctor Berkley said, and nodding to the housekeeper, who appeared entirely astonished by this revelation, he led Grace from the house.

A NEW HOME

"Ah, yes, I don't usually eat breakfast. I'm a little disorganised, I'm afraid, Grace," Doctor Berkley said, looking somewhat embarrassed as he cleared a pile of papers from the top of the kitchen table.

Grace had spent her first night at the doctor's cottage sleeping in a bed in the attic, made up beneath the eaves. She and Doctor Berkley had eaten a simple dinner of soused herring and buttered bread, but the doctor had been called out to assist with a birth in a neighbouring village and had not returned until well after midnight.

"It's all right, I can make the breakfast," Grace said, for she had watched Mrs. Lewes prepare Lady Edith's breakfast tray often enough and knew how to make tea and toast crumpets and muffins over the fire.

Doctor Berkley looked at her and smiled.

"You don't need to be my maid, Grace. That's not why you're here. I've always managed well enough on my own, you see, but... well, I suppose things have to change," he said, and Grace smiled.

"I don't mind. I'm used to helping my mother and Lady Edith–I was..." she said, her words trailing off.

Doctor Berkley nodded.

"I think there's some damson jam in the cupboard, and the remnants of a loaf of bread. We can stoke up the fire and boil some water for the tea. There might even be some eggs if the hens are feeling generous. Why don't I go and see?" he said.

Grace nodded. She could only be grateful to Doctor Berkley for his kindness towards her and was only too willing to assist him with domestic tasks. It was not long before the kettle was whistling, and several pieces of bread had been toasted over the embers of the fire.

The hens *had* laid, and Doctor Berkley fried two of the eggs in a frying pan on the grate. With the tea made, and the table cleared, they sat down to a pleasant breakfast, the storm clouds of the previous day now replaced with a bright, sunny, but cold morning, the frost making patterns on the windows, and lying thick across the garden.

"What delicious jam," Grace said, as she spread another slice of toast thickly with the tart conserve.

"A grateful patient–she claimed I cured her of gout. I've received a pot every month for the past year," the doctor replied, shaking his head and laughing.

"Do you have patients to see today?" Grace asked.

She was curious about the doctor's work. Grace had always watched her mother at her duties, and it was her own ambition to be a nurse one day, too.

"I do, yes, and I'd better get going. I've got my rounds–house calls, and the baby from last night to check on. It was a boy–a real bruiser of a child, eight pounds," Doctor Berkley said, shaking his head.

He rose to his feet and took up his medical bag. Grace felt suddenly emboldened. She did not want to remain all day at the cottage with nothing to do, and she now asked the doctor a question she had wanted to ask before but had never had the courage to do so.

"Might I come with you, Doctor Berkley? I'd like to see what you do. I always watched my mother, and she always told what she was doing. I know I'm only young, but I do so want to be a nurse," Grace said.

Doctor Berkley looked surprised, but he did not immediately dismiss the idea out of hand.

"Well... are you sure? I don't know how interesting you'd find it. I'm going to see Mrs. Wilks–the widow who lives in the cottage on the hill above the village. She's suffering from terrible headaches. And then I'm due at the Fosters. Their boy, Pritch, has an ulcer in his mouth–he's bitten his cheek. Then I'll go and see the baby. You can come with me, but..." he hesitated, even as Grace nodded.

"I'd like that. I'd like it very much," she said, feeling suddenly excited at the prospect of helping the doctor in his duties.

It was not long before they were walking up Howard's Hill, a strange landmark amidst the flatness of the surrounding countryside, on the top of which, in a small cottage, lived Mrs. Wilks, a widow whose husband had been a fisherman.

"She can be somewhat irritable, though if one's in pain, it's hardly surprising. It's hard to know what's wrong with her, though I suspect she forgets to drink and becomes unwell as a result. I've prescribed her willow tea in the hope of reminding her to drink, though I'm not sure I've been terribly successful in my ministrations," Doctor Berkley said, as they made their way up the overgrown garden path.

The walls of the cottage were covered in dead ivy and wisteria, and the roof was badly in need of repair. The door was ajar, and Doctor Berkley knocked, waiting for the reply, which came in the form of a loud voice from upstairs.

"It's on the latch. Let yourself in," Mrs. Wilks called out.

"It's Doctor Berkley, Mrs. Wilks. I've come to see about your headaches," the doctor replied.

They stepped inside, and several cats shot out into the garden, mewing and hissing. The hallway was small and cramped. An unpleasant smell hung in the air, and the cottage was messy, the remnants of a meal standing on a table in the parlour, whilst the stairs were strewn with dirty clothes.

"I'm upstairs, Doctor Berkley," Mrs. Wilks shouted, and the doctor beckoned Grace to follow him.

They made their way upstairs to the landing, where a door stood open, revealing Mrs. Wilks lying in bed. She was a large woman, her breathing heavy and erratic, and her face was bright red, peering out from under a white cloth nightcap, the blankets pulled up to her chin.

"How are you feeling today, Mrs. Wilks?" Doctor Berkley asked, approaching the bed, as Grace stood in the doorway.

"What's she doing here? Who's she?" Mrs. Wilks demanded, staring at Grace, who felt suddenly out of place.

But Doctor Berkley appeared unconcerned with his patient's angry tone.

"Oh, that's my assistant, Grace. You'll be seeing more of her in the weeks and months to come, Mrs. Wilks. Now, tell me, have you been drinking the willow tea–the medicine I prescribed for you?" the doctor asked.

"It tastes funny. I don't like it," Mrs. Wilks replied.

"It was never meant to taste nice, Mrs. Wilks. Medicines usually don't. Never mind, we can but persevere, don't you think? I want you to keep taking it and be sure to drink plenty of fluids, too. The more you drink, the more your headaches will ease. You're not drinking enough. That's what's causing your headaches," Doctor Berkley said, and Mrs. Wilks looked at him sulkily.

"It's hard to get out of bed, doctor. It's so cold in the house, and I've got no one but myself," she said.

Grace felt sorry for her, and Doctor Berkley nodded.

"I'll speak to the curate. There might be someone who could come and help you–a girl from the village, perhaps. We'll look into it. I'll call on you in two days. Keep drinking, Mrs. Wilks," he said, rising to his feet and patting her hand.

Mrs. Wilks glanced at Grace and tutted.

"Send your assistant to help me," she said, but Doctor Berkley shook his head.

"Oh, I don't think so, Mrs. Wilks. She's still got far too much to learn," he said, winking at Grace, as he hurried her out of the room and down the stairs.

As they left the cottage a moment later, Doctor Berkley began to laugh.

"What's so funny?" Grace asked, for she had felt terribly sorry for Mrs. Wilks, lying there all alone with a terrible headache.

"Oh, I'm sorry, Grace–but the woman does nothing to help herself. She won't take her medicines. She won't do what I tell her to do. She's perfectly capable of getting out of bed. There's nothing wrong with her. Not really. All she does is complain and expect a miracle cure, with no effort on her part. It's a fundamental rule of medicine, Grace. The patient has to want to get better. I don't mean they can will it for themselves, but they need to want it, and Mrs. Wilks is quite happy as an invalid. That's my diagnosis. Come now, let's go and see the Fosters–it's a nasty ulcer the boy's got," Doctor Berkley said, as they hurried down Howard's Hill back towards the village.

The rest of the day was spent in the pleasant–and less pleasant–pursuit of a country doctor's duties. The ulcer was bathed with salt solution, the new baby was checked over and weighed again, a case of measles was identified, and a twisted ankle was set. Grace watched in fascination as Doctor Berkley went diligently about his duties.

He was unfailingly kind, and was always thanked profusely when he left whichever dwelling he had entered to provide his ministrations. Grace watched, always introduced as the doctor's assistant, and there were many in the village who knew her story and commiserated with her over the death of Lady Edith.

"You were a good companion to her. She spoke lovingly of you," the curate's sister, who had twisted her ankle in the rose garden of the rectory, commented, and others said the same.

At the end of the day, Grace and Doctor Berkley were about to return home, when Grace remembered she still had her things to collect from Carshalton House. She had been so caught up in the interests and intrigues of the day as to have quite forgotten the unpleasant business awaiting her.

"We'll go now and get it over with," Doctor Berkley said, and they set off through the woods towards the house.

Lamps were burning in the study as they crossed the gardens, and through the windows, Grace could see Captain Dickinson pacing back and forth in front of the fire. She wondered what he was doing, what he was thinking and whether he would remain in Norfolk or return to London.

"Surely, he won't stay here for long," Grace said, voicing her thoughts as they approached the kitchen door.

"I don't know what he'll do. I can't imagine there's much attraction in remaining in Norfolk–especially in the winter when the storms blow in," Doctor Berkley replied.

The kitchen door now opened, and Mrs. Parks appeared, holding Grace's meagre possessions, trussed up in a blanket.

"And good riddance to you. I don't know why you've taken her in, doctor. I really don't. She belongs in an orphanage or a poorhouse," the housekeeper said, handing over the bundle to Grace, who took it and stepped back.

"That's my business, Mrs. Parks. And on my part, I hope never to darken the door of this house again–not whilst it remains under such... unfortunate occupation," Doctor Berkley replied.

Mrs. Parks' eyes grew wide with anger, and she turned and

slammed the door in their faces. Doctor Berkley smiled.

"I'm glad I don't have to stay there any longer," Grace said, as Doctor Berkley took the bundle from her and led her back towards the gardens.

"I'm sure you are—wicked woman," he said.

They were just crossing the lawn when the sound of a window being pulled up came from behind, and the voice of Captain Dickinson called out to them.

"You won't get anything, you know—be gone with you. I've told that fool Fletcher to do all he can to close the clause. I'll get the money back, you see if I don't. You get nothing," he shouted.

Grace turned, finding the angry face of the captain looking out at her. But with Doctor Berkley at her side, and having escaped the cruelty of Mrs. Parks, she felt suddenly emboldened.

"I loved Lady Edith, and I don't care what you say. I know she loved me, too—and my mother," she cried out.

"Bah! Nonsense. The two of you were in on it together. You and your wicked mother. If she hadn't died, she'd have been the one taking the money," the captain called back.

"I don't care about the money. I don't want the money," Grace replied.

It was true. Apart from repaying Doctor Berkley for his kindness, the thought of the money was of no consequence. Grace had always had nothing, and she would gladly have swapped the money for just another day with her mother or Lady Edith.

"And what do you plan to do, foolish child? Without money, what can you be?" Captain Dickinson demanded.

Grace thought for a moment, unperturbed by the possibility of the captain's threat, and in a clear and definite voice, she replied.

"I'm going to be a nurse," she said, looking up at Doctor Berkley and smiling.

PART II

A COUNTRY PRACTICE

S *pring 1870*

     "Don't walk on it for a few days, Miss Langford. You'll have to let your father do the bulk of the planting," Doctor Berkley said, rising to his feet, as the patient moved her twisted ankle awkwardly.

"Oh, dear. We'll be so behind," she said, shaking her head.

"It'll heel quicker the less you do with it, Miss Langford," Grace said, and the patient looked at her and smiled.

"Do you remember when I fell out of the tree during the apple harvest? You said just the same thing. I was lucky not to break anything, but I was bruised black and blue all over, wasn't I?" she said, and Grace nodded.

"You certainly were. We used a whole bottle of witch hazel on you," Grace said, and Miss Langford laughed.

"I can still smell it," she said, as Doctor Berkley closed his medical bag.

"Very good. Well, try to rest, Miss Langford. I know it's not easy when there's so much to do, but I'm sure you'll manage. Come now, Grace, we need to prepare some ointments. We're running rather low on our stocks. Good day, Miss Langford," the doctor called out.

Grace was now twelve years old and had been Doctor Berkley's assistant ever since she had left Carshalton Lodge. She went with him wherever he went, watching him treat coughs and colds, broken bones, headaches, sicknesses of the stomach, and every other malady imaginable in young and old alike.

He delivered babies, tended the dying, and had even been known to put his talents at the services of the local farmers when one of their animals fell ill. He was a respected physician, and welcomed everywhere in the village, save at Carshalton House, where he received only an icy reception on the few occasions he was called to minister to one of the servants.

"She's always doing some injury to herself," Grace said, as they made their way along the lane from the farm where Miss Langford lived with her father, Morris.

"And he's getting no younger, either. I just hope she listens to my advice, that's all," Doctor Berkley replied, and Grace laughed. Miss Langford never listened to advice.

"I'm sure she might sit still for a few moments–if we're lucky," she said, and Doctor Berkley rolled his eyes.

Grace, too, was well known in the village. She was well liked, and whilst Doctor Berkley's bedside manner could occasionally be somewhat brusque, her own was gentle and nurse like. She had inherited that from her mother and was only too glad to be doing that which she had always imagined and hoped she one day would.

Grace wanted to be a nurse, or even a doctor, though she knew the profession was closed to her, something Doctor Berkley had told her when she had asked him as to the possibility.

"Only men can be doctors, Grace. But nursing is a good and worthy profession, though not everyone thinks so," he had told her.

But for now, Grace was content to watch Doctor Berkley at his work, keen to learn as much as she could from him and determined to prove herself worthy of the work she intended to do.

"Now, we're low on almost everything. It's so hard to get things brought out here. We must make do with what we've got," Doctor Berkley said, as they approached the cottage.

"I can get started. I know the mixtures–we've plenty of powders. We can mix a simple ointment," Grace said, but as she was speaking, Doctor Berkley let out an exasperated exclamation.

"Oh, goodness me, I've left my medical bag at the Langford farm. I'll have to go back and get it. Yes, you get started, Grace, and if you might make me something to eat for my return. It's been a long day," the doctor said, and scolding himself, he hurried back in the direction of the farm.

Grace smiled. Doctor Berkley was always forgetting things. He had been a kind and patient guardian, even as he would be the first to admit he knew nothing about raising children. But the two of them had forged a strong bond, and Grace had come to love the doctor as a father, just as he loved her as a daughter.

"Poor Doctor Berkley. He's always forgetting something," Grace thought to herself, smiling as she made her way through the garden gate and up the path to the cottage.

Spring was in the air, and the garden was bursting into bloom, the damp scent of earth and new growth hanging in the air, mixed with the salty taste of the sea. Grace could hear the waves crashing on the rocks at the mouth of the ravine.

This part of the coast was treacherous, and there had been many ships wrecked on the rocks, their cargos washed up on the beach, and many lives lost. It made Grace shudder to think of it, and now she let herself into the cottage, ready to make up the ointments she and Doctor Berkley needed for their rounds.

"Willow bark, and what else? Witch hazel... do we still have the

chamomile?" Grace asked herself, peering at the various half-empty bottles on the shelves.

She had just taken down a jar of opium pills when she heard footsteps hurrying up the path, and a frantic knocking came at the door.

"Doctor Berkley? Are you in?" a voice came from outside, and Grace hurried to open it.

She found one of the grooms from Carshalton House standing on the step, breathless and red faced. His name was John Crawshaw, a young man of around eighteen or nineteen, whom Grace had known when he was younger.

"What's wrong? What's happened?" Grace exclaimed.

"It's William Hunter. He's fallen from one of the horses in the stable yard. He's in a bad way. I think his leg's broken. Where's Doctor Berkley? He needs to come quickly," John exclaimed.

Grace knew it would take the doctor at least half an hour to return from the Langford farm. Miss Langford would keep him talking, and if her father was there, he would do so, too.

"He's not here, but I can help. I know what to do," Grace said, seizing the emergency bag the doctor kept by the door for just such an occasion.

It contained splints, bandages, ointments, and remedies for all manner of ailments, ready to be snatched up in a moment. The groom looked at her doubtfully.

"You? But you're just his assistant, aren't you?" he said, but Grace shook her head.

"He needs tending to immediately. I can help. Doctor Berkley isn't here. I'll leave him a note. He'll come as soon as he returns, but there's no time to waste," Grace replied, and she hurried John along the path, knowing she could help.

The groomsman had been too young to find himself embroiled in the circumstances of Grace's departure from the house, and she shared no animosity with either him or William, both of whom were good and honest men. As they approached the stables, Grace could hear the injured groom moaning in agony, and she found him lying in the stable yard, his leg twisted in a terrible contortion.

"Where's the doctor?" he groaned, as Grace kneeled at his side.

"He's coming, but I can help you. We need to set the leg. It needs a splint," she said, having watched Doctor Berkley do so dozens of times.

William was moaning in pain, delirious, almost, and Grace instructed John to help her, as she made William bite on a piece of wood, ready to move the leg back into its natural position. Time was of the essence, and despite John's reluctantance, Grace insisted on his helping her.

"But shouldn't we wait?" the groom asked, but Grace shook her head.

"The longer we wait, the harder it'll be. The leg needs to return to its right position. Come now, help me," she insisted, and showing John where to grasp, she counted to three, moving leg, just as she knew Doctor Berkley himself would have done.

William's face was red with pain, and sweat was pouring from his brow. His eyes were wide with agony, but the leg was back in its proper position, and Grace now made it secure with the splint, tying the knots as Doctor Berkley had shown her. Removing the block of wood from William's mouth, the groom let out a deep sigh, lying back and crying out in agony.

"My goodness, what pain! I can hardly bear it," he exclaimed, just as footsteps on the cobbles announced the arrival of Doctor Berkley himself.

He looked down at the scene before him in astonishment, raising his eyebrows, as Grace turned to look at him.

"I've set the leg and made the splint secure. There wasn't time to wait for you. I came at once when John called at the cottage," Grace said, as Doctor Berkley stooped down to examine her handiwork.

He smiled and shook his head.

"You've done remarkably well. The knots are perfect, and you've splinted the leg dead straight. I couldn't have done it better myself," he said, glancing up at William, whose face was still red with pain, and his brow sweaty.

"Is it badly broken, doctor? I fell from the horse. I was just trotting her, and she bucked," he said.

"It looks bad, yes, William. But it'll heal–in time. You've been lucky to receive the ministrations of an excellent physician, and I don't mean myself," he said.

John shook his head and laughed.

"Well, William–there's a fine thing. Your leg set by a child. What are you, Grace, twelve years old?" he asked, and Grace nodded.

"She might be twelve years old, but she knows just what she's doing, I assure you," Doctor Berkley replied.

It took several of the servants from the house–two footmen and a hall boy, along with John and Doctor Berkley to lift the groom and carry him into the stable quarters where he was laid on a bed.

"When will I ride again, doctor?" William asked, and Doctor Berkley looked at him sympathetically.

"When your leg heals, William, and only time will tell when that is," he replied.

Grace and Doctor Berkley left the groom to his lamentations, stepping out into the sunshine bathing the stable yard in a warm glow. Doctor Berkley turned to Grace and smiled.

"When I read your note, I was a little angry. I didn't believe you could do it, but I meant it when I said you'd set the leg just as I'd have done. You've exceeded my expectations, Grace. You really have," Doctor Berkley said, and Grace smiled.

"I... I knew I could do it. I've seen you do it so many times, and I knew there wasn't time to wait. It had to be done there and then. John helped me lift the limb, but I knew how to splint the break and give him some relief from the pain–only a little, of course," Grace replied.

Instinct had taken over, and Grace had known just what to do, performing her duties just as her mother might have done in her place. Doctor Berkley placed his hand on her shoulder.

"I'm proud of you, Grace. You've learned so much. It's a joy to see it, and I'm sure William's grateful, too," he replied.

Grace smiled. No one had believed she could do it, but she had proved them wrong, and now she was determined to show more of the skills she had learned from watching Doctor Berkley at work.

"I'm glad I could help him," Grace replied, slipping her hand into Doctor Berkley's, as the two of them returned home.

* * *

Two days later, the grocer's boy, Edmund, arrived at the cottage with a large tin of toffees. The note was addressed to Grace, thanking her for her kindness in helping William in his hour of need.

"They're from him and his mother," Grace said, opening the tin and offering it to Doctor Berkley, who took one of the brightly wrapped sweets and smiled.

"Your first gift of thanks. We won't charge for our services. I'm sure these toffees won't be the last gift we receive from William and his mother in lieu of payment. What a kind gesture, and you should be very proud of yourself, Grace. You proved yourself a worthy successor to your mother. Healing must be in your blood. I'm a firm believer in it. My father was a physician, and my grandfather a naval surgeon. He sawed off limbs whilst cannon fire raged all around him," Doctor Berkley said, with a cheery smile.

During the winter months, Grace had not visited her mother's grave, but with no house calls to make that morning, she took a handful of toffees and made her way through the woods to the churchyard. Finding her mother's grave somewhat overgrown, with flowers growing beneath the headstones. Large white daisies with yellow centres seemed to smile at her as she cleared the surrounding weeds away.

"I'm sorry I haven't been to see you for a while, Mother," Grace said, sitting down in front of the gravestone, the words of which were covered in moss and lichen.

She reached out to scrape at the words, tracing the craving with her fingers. The stone had been paid for by Lady Edith, and was tucked away at the far end of the churchyard, beneath an overhanging oak tree, the boughs of which reached down to make a shady canopy for the grave, set apart as it was from the other stones.

"I'm still helping Doctor Berkley. You'd have been proud of me. I set a broken leg in a splint. It was William–a groom at Carshalton House. He sent me a tin of toffees as a thank you. I've got some here," Grace said, rummaging in her pocket and bringing out the brightly wrapped sweets.

A gentle breeze was blowing through the trees, and Grace sat for a while by her mother's grave, talking to her about all things she had learned since the last time she had visited the grave.

Doctor Berkley was always teaching her something new, and she had learned more than she had ever thought possible. There was a school in the village, and Grace attended as her duties allowed, though the schoolmaster, Mr. Dixon, acknowledged she learned far more from Doctor Berkley than from him.

"Though you'll never be a doctor. You realise that, don't you, Grace?" he had said, and Grace had told him she did, even as it pained her to admit it.

Doctors were men, and Grace knew becoming a doctor was

an impossibility, even as she dreamed of it every day. She sat for an hour or so by her mother's grave, having cleared off most of the moss and lichen by the time she rose to her feet.

"Well, goodbye, Mother. I'll come again soon, I promise," she said, kissing the palm of her hand and placing it on the rough, worn headstone.

Her mother had always kissed her on the forehead when she was a child, and it felt to Grace as though she was now doing the same, bidding her mother goodbye, as now she crossed the churchyard to the plot where Lady Edith was buried.

Her stone, too–a far grander affair in marble–stood neglected. Captain Dickinson never visited, and the only person to lay flowers there was Grace herself. She had picked a posy of wildflowers from the hedgerow by the cottage, and now she laid them on Lady Edith's grave, brushing away a tear as she thought of the two women she loved the most, both resting in the churchyard.

I miss them both so very much," Grace thought to herself, even as she knew how fortunate she was to have Doctor Berkley as her guardian.

Again, she lingered a while by the grave, thinking through all the things she would have told Lady Edith had she been alive to hear them. She, too, would have been astonished at the story of the splintered leg, and would surely have applauded Grace for her efforts. But now it was time to leave, and Grace reluctantly said goodbye, walking through the long grass of the churchyard to leave by the gate leading into the woodland, the path turning left to Carshalton House, and right towards the village.

As she turned to walk down into the ravine, Grace saw two people ahead. The unmistakable figure of Mrs. Parks and that of Dolby Cleverley, the gardener who had plotted with the house-keeper to steal Lady Edith's jewels. They were deep in conversation, and did not notice Grace, who hurriedly hid behind the nearest tree.

"We just need to wait for a storm. I've seen lots of ships passing this past month, but there's never been the right moment for it," Dolby was saying, and Grace listened, curious to know what they were talking about.

"Captain Dickinson said the same. It's just a matter of waiting. At least we know where to give the signal from," Mrs. Parks replied.

They walked within a few feet of Grace's hiding place, their words now lost amongst the trees. Grace was curious. She did not know why the housekeeper and the gardener should be discussing the possibility of a storm out at sea.

The storms along the coast were notorious, and when they came, the villagers would retreat into their houses and weather out the onslaught of driving rain and strong wind. But as Grace emerged back onto the path, she could not help but feel a sense of unease, as though once again she had overheard something the housekeeper would wish to keep a secret, and as she hurried back to the cottage, she was resolved to tell Doctor Berkley everything she had overheard.

STRANGE LIGHTS

"*I*'ve suspected as much in the past," Doctor Berkley said, after Grace had told him what she had overheard the housekeeper and gardener discussing.

"But what do they mean to do?" Grace asked, for she was still confused as to the intention lying behind the words.

"They're going to cause a wreck. It's a notorious coastline, very dangerous. Ships can be lured onto the rocks by lights shone from the shore. A captain might presume it to be a lighthouse guiding them to safety, but when he sails in closer, he hits the rocks. All hands are lost, or most of them, and the cargo washes up on the shore to be collected by the wreckers. It's a nasty business, Grace, very nasty, indeed," Doctor Berkley replied, shaking his head.

The thought of it made Grace shudder, even as she was hardly surprised to think of Mrs. Parks being capable of such wickedness. There had been other wrecks in the past, just as Doctor Berkley described, and Grace remembered the housekeeper speaking gleefully of the things she had found on the beach. But Grace had never suspected her of being part of a plot to cause the wrecks.

"But... oh, it's too horrible. Do they really mean to wreck a ship? Why doesn't someone stop them?" Grace asked, and Doctor Berkley sighed.

"This is a lonely place, Grace. We're far from the authorities and the magistrates. And when a whole village is involved..." he said, his words trailing off, as he glanced out of the window.

"The whole village?" Grace asked, and Doctor Berkley nodded.

"I've always suspected it. Mrs. Wilks might like me to think she's an invalid, but I'm certain she watches for incoming ships from her cottage, just as her late husband did, too. I've seen the flash of a light from there on stormy nights, as though she's signalling to someone about an approaching ship. And the Langfords, too. The barns at their farm are the perfect place to store whatever might be found on the beach. Even the curate, he's been here a very long time. It's not exactly a plum living, but he seems wealthy enough," Doctor Berkley said.

Grace had never imagined the meekly mannered villagers to be capable of such a thing. Mrs. Parks was different, and the servants at Carshalton House, too, but not the curate or old Mrs. Wilks or the Langfords.

"Do you really think so, Doctor Berkley?" Grace said, and the doctor nodded.

"I do, Grace, as much as it seems unpalatable to think it. But I'm worried now–its seems they're waiting for a storm to come," he said, glancing out of the window.

The day was bright and sunny, but Grace knew how easily the weather could change. A storm could blow up out at sea and bring with it waves as high as the cliffs themselves. She shuddered at the thought of the flashing light drawing an unsuspecting ship into danger.

"What can we do to stop them?" Grace asked.

"We can be vigilant. I managed to stop one once. You were

young then, and fast asleep. I noticed a light flashing on the headland, and I hurried out into the storm to head them off. From the
far side of the ravine, there's a place to hide. I flashed a light from
there, and by the grace of God, it was my light and not that of the
wreckers the ship followed. They sailed wide of the rocks and on
to safety. But if I hadn't succeeded..." he said, his words trailing off.

Grace had never suspected the mild-mannered doctor of
being so brave, and she felt relieved to think they had discovered the workings of another plot before it was too late.

"I want to help. I want to stop them," Grace said, but Doctor
Berkley sighed.

"I was lucky that night, but I haven't always been. You've
heard of the wrecks along this coast. It's famous for them, or
notorious. But it's all the work of the wreckers. There's nothing
dangerous about these waters, only those who inhabit the land,"
he said, shaking his head.

Grace reached out and put his hand on hers. They were
sitting at the table in the parlour, surrounded by the instruments and medicines the doctor used to save lives, even as those
around him were plotting to take them.

"We'll keep watch. I'll stay up. I can watch from the attic
window. I can see the headland from there. If a storm comes,
we'll know to be ready. We can flash the light from the far side
of the ravine–just as you did before," Grace said.

Doctor Berkley looked sceptical.

"I fear it won't work. It won't be easy to be so vigilant. I was
lucky before, but I've been unfortunate, too," he said, shaking
his head.

But Grace was determined to try. Mrs. Parks had already
taken so much from her, and she was not about to allow the
housekeeper to take innocent lives, too. She thought of her
mother, knowing she, too, would be brave in such circumstances.

"We've got to try, Doctor Berkley. We've got to wait for the storm," she said.

* * *

THEY DID NOT HAVE long to wait. Spring that year had been unusually warm, and the rumble of thunder had often echoed across the flat Norfolk plains. Grace and Doctor Berkley went about their duties, mindful of the wickedness simmering under the surface of village life. An evil lurking in the hearts of so many.

"Good morning, Mr. Sanderson," Doctor Berkley said as the familiar figure of the curate appeared around the bend of the lane leading to Mrs. Wilks' cottage.

"Ah, Doctor Berkeley, good morning. A fine day, though it looks like rain later. These thunderstorms have been quite dreadful. My sister hides all the silver spoons whenever she hears a rumble–she's terrified of lightning. I rather like it," he said, smiling at Grace, who returned his smile with a blank gaze.

He was an elderly man, his white hair parted in the centre, and wore a pair of half-moon spectacles, his high collar identifying him as a tractarian–the village church having been turned over to certain high church notions, unpalatable to some and embraced by others.

"Did you find Mrs. Wilks well?" Doctor Berkley asked.

"Oh, yes... we were talking about spiritual matters," the curate replied.

"She has a steely determination to continue, despite her many ailments," Doctor Berkley said, and the curate nodded.

"Yes, I agree. She'll outlive us all. Well, I must get on. The storm's coming," he said, and nodding to Doctor Berkley, he hurried off down the path.

"Spiritual matters? I imagine we'll find Mrs. Wilks in rude health, and with a lamp at her side," Doctor Berkley whispered.

Mrs. Wilks was, indeed, in rude health, and she practically dismissed Doctor Berkley out of hand, telling him she wanted to rest, rather than be disturbed by his ministrations. Grace and the doctor returned home, and Grace went at once to the attic, where she made preparations for the watch.

"It's going to happen tonight–they must know there's a ship due to sail past," Grace said, as the first drops of rain now pattered against the cottage windows.

It had been warm that day, the clouds gathering on the horizon, and low rumbles of thunder echoing across the Norfolk countryside. The rain now grew heavier, and Grace and Doctor Berkley ate a hurried dinner of bread and cheese, before Grace returned to her vantage point, watching as it grew dark outside.

The rain was heavier now, and in the last of the fading daylight, Grace could see the waves rising and crashing on the rocks at the mouth of the ravine. It was going to be a spectacular storm.

"Anything yet?" Doctor Berkley asked, as he brought Grace a cup of cocoa later that evening.

She turned and shook her head. Everything was in darkness, the only light coming from the village inn, where a lamp burned above the door.

Out to sea, Grace could see nothing, though she could hear the waves crashing against the rocks, and the rain was driving against the windows. Any ship at sea would be glad of a guiding light on such a night, even as it made Grace shudder to think of it.

"Nothing. I can only see the lamp above the door of the inn. That's all," she said, taking the cup of cocoa from him.

He came to the window and peered out into the darkness, shaking his head and sighing.

"Perhaps we'll be fortunate–perhaps they'll not take the risk. It's dangerous for them, too," he said, but as he spoke, a light suddenly appeared on the headline.

"Look!" Grace exclaimed, peering through the darkness, as a flash came and went.

"There's the signal. That's it," Doctor Berkley said, and he clattered down the stairs from the attic, with Grace following behind.

Everything was ready. They had their own lamp, a tinder box, and a sheet to cover it and lift from it to make it flash. Hurrying out of the cottage, they found themselves in the midst of a deluge, and ran into the trees, following the path leading to the far side of the ravine opposite the headland.

The wind roared, and the waves crashed on the rocks below. Grace had never seen such a storm, and as they came to the point along the path where they could see out to sea, the awesomeness of the storm became apparent.

Lightning flashed across the sky, lighting up the waves, cascading onto the rocks. Their spray was as high as the height of the ravine, and Grace could taste the salty water on her lips as Doctor Berkley hurried to light the lamp.

"Let me help you," Grace said, and she held up the sheet, protecting the flame from the wind. The lamp was lit, but even as Doctor Berkley held it up, the light on the headland flashed again.

"They're trying to draw it onto the rocks. There's nothing we can do now but hope they'll follow out light and not theirs. It's up to the captain," Doctor Berkley said.

As another flash of lightning lit up the sky, Grace saw the ship itself. She was a cargo vessel, tossing and turning amidst the waves, her sails billowing in the ferocious wind, and one of her masts damaged.

"There's the ship. It's sailing close to the shore," Grace said, holding out the sheet to flash the light Doctor Berkley held up.

"Too close, it's following the wreckers' light. It'll be dashed on the rocks. Fools!" he exclaimed, as another flash came from the headland.

As the scene was again illuminated by the lightning, Grace saw the ship floundering. They had been too late, and now it was sailing towards the rocks, certain to be dashed to pieces. Doctor Berkley threw down the lamp and cursed.

"What can we do?" Grace asked, but as she spoke, a terrible noise, louder than the wind itself, rend the air.

The sound was that of the ship hitting the rocks–scraping, creaking, splitting–and Grace could do nothing but watch helplessly as each flash of lightning brought with it the unfolding of that dreadful scene.

The ship was split in two, its bow and stern both upended, the rocks piercing through its hull. The second mast fell, crashing into the waters below. But the most horrific sight was that of the crew jumping into the water, where the waves caught them and pulled them under. Some could swim, but others were helpless as now they tried to reach the safety of the rocks at the foot of the ravine.

"My God. What wickedness!" Doctor Berkley exclaimed, and he seized Grace by the hand, hurrying her back through the trees and along the path leading to the village.

"Where are we going?" Grace asked.

"To help them, of course. We can get down to the rocks by the harbour wall. If we hurry, we might save some of them. The wreckers have done their job. They'll wait until morning to collect their spoils," he said, and sure enough, Grace saw a party of people, their outlines silhouetted by the flashes of lightning, hurrying along the headland.

She could not tell if Mrs. Parks, or Dolby, or even the curate were amongst them. But whoever was responsible for shining the light–and it seemed the whole village had played its part–they had blood on their hands.

"Wait, Doctor Berkley. It's too dangerous," Grace called out, as the doctor now picked his way down onto the rocks below the harbour.

Cries for help were coming from the water below, and it seemed no one had yet reached the safety of the shore. Grace could not swim, and she held back as Doctor Berkley disappeared from sight.

"What's happening? What's going on?" a voice from behind called out, and Grace turned to find the landlord of the village inn, Joe Perkins, standing behind her, holding a lamp in his hand.

He was joined by several others, and Grace pointed towards the water.

"A ship's been wrecked. There're survivors in the water. Doctor Berkley's trying to help them," Grace replied.

For a moment, she feared the landlord could be part of the conspiracy, but the grim look on his face suggested otherwise, and he shook his head, turning to the others and urging them to assist.

"Damn wreckers. Quickly, get the lifeboat, we can save some of them—God help us to save them all. The doctor shouldn't have gone in alone, though," the landlord said, hurrying to the harbour side.

He called out Doctor Berkley's name in the darkness, but there was no reply—only the howling of the wind and the desperate cries of the men in the water. The lifeboat was an old, rickety craft, also used for fishing, and the men who had accompanied the landlord now appeared from a nearby boat shed, their cork buoyancy aids around their shoulders, and heaving the boat down the slip into the raging torrent below.

Grace could do nothing but watch, and the landlord, too, leaped into the boat, urging the men into the water.

"Doctor Berkley?" Grace called out, but there was still no reply.

She made her way cautiously along the rocks, the spray soaking her to the skin, as the waves crashed below. Another bright flash of lightning lit up the air, and in the water, Grace could see several dozen men, all crying out for help, unable to swim in the rise and swell of the storm.

The ship itself was entirely lost, and would only be reachable in the morning, when the tide went out. Grace could see it on the rocks at the end of the headland, its broken bow exposed to the driving rain still hampering the rescue efforts.

"Look lively there, reach that man–pull him in," the landlord was shouting, and again, Grace called out for Doctor Berkley, her voice lost on the wind, which howled across the sea.

She had gone as far as she dared, and now she stood alone on the rocks, tears welling up in her eyes, salty like the sea.

"Doctor Berkley? Where are you? Can you hear me?" she called out, but there was no reply–only the howling wind, the driving rain, and the desperate cries of dying men.

WRECKED LIVES

*T*he morning was still. The calm after the storm. The tide had gone out, leaving a vast expanse of sand reaching out beyond the headland where gentle waves lapped at its peripheries. The lifeboat had returned to shore, and only five of the twenty-five strong crew had been rescued.

The rest, including the captain, were missing, presumed dead, drowned by the actions of the wreckers, who had so wilfully shone their light the night before.

"It's a wicked business," the landlord said, shaking his head.

But that did not stop the villagers from hurrying across the sand towards the wrecked ship. It was marooned on rocks at the far point of the headland, and all around it lay the spoils of destruction.

The cargo ship had been carrying barrels of rum and whisky, along with all manner of goods bound for Edinburgh. There was no telling who amongst the crowd was responsible for wrecking the ship, and Grace saw Mrs. Parks and Dolby gleefully helping themselves to the contents of a chest containing tobacco and tea.

"I hope the water's spoiled it," she thought to herself, but Grace had other matters on her mind.

There was still no sign of Doctor Berkley. Many of the bodies of the sailors had been washed up on the shore, lying at intervals on the sand. Those villagers with a conscience were making slow progress of collecting them, whilst others hurried past for their own gain–the servants of Carshalton House amongst them.

"I don't know where Doctor Berkley is. I've not seen him since he went into the water," Grace said, and the landlord looked at her gravely.

"You should prepare for the worst, Grace. We're still finding bodies. He was a fool to go into the water, but a brave fool, nonetheless," the landlord replied.

Tears welled up in Grace's eyes, but she refused to believe the doctor was dead–not until she had seen it with her own eyes. She watched as another body was brought onto the harbour wall. It was that of a young boy, perhaps only the same age as Grace herself. His face was pale, his eyes closed, and his shirt torn. Such a loss of life, and all for the price of a few barrels of rum and boxes of tobacco.

"We tried to stop them. We shone a light from the woods above the ravine. Doctor Berkley said it would bring the ship to safety if they followed it. But they didn't," Grace said, looking out towards the shipwreck, and imagining the horror of those on board as they realised the inevitability of disaster.

"And now the vultures gather," the landlord said, shaking his head as he returned to the grim task of collecting the bodies.

Grace wanted to help. She wanted to do something, anything, to assist in finding Doctor Berkley. She clung to hope, even as every passing moment seemed more hopeless. As another body was brought up onto the harbour wall, the sound of a carriage was heard outside the inn, and Grace turned to find Captain Dickinson alighting, and Mrs. Parks hurrying to greet him.

"It's quite a wreck, sir, she was badly damaged. They'll never repair her. And the whole beach, it's covered with the haul," she said, hardly bothering to disguise the glee in her voice.

"A remarkable sight, Mrs. Parks," the captain said, shaking his head.

Grace was disgusted. She knew it was their doing–for Captain Dickinson, too, surely had a hand in it.

"And I suppose you're here playing the nurse, are you? Where's the doctor?" Captain Dickinson called out, beckoning Grace over to him.

Mrs. Parks stood sneering at his side.

"He went out to help rescue the survivors of the wreck. I haven't seen him since," Grace replied.

Captain Dickinson looked momentarily surprised, and even Mrs. Parks looked somewhat perturbed.

"You think he's dead?" she asked, and Grace shook her head.

"I won't believe it until I see it. I'm hopeful..." she said, but at these words, a cry came from the harbour wall, and the landlord beckoned Grace over.

"I think we've found him," he said, and Grace hurried over, watching as a body was lifted from the rocks close to the wreck. She let out a cry, recognising the clothes Doctor Berkley had been wearing. It was him, and before anyone could stop her, she had run down to the sands and across to where the other rescuers were carrying the body. Tears were rolling down her cheeks, and she flung herself down, clutching at the doctor's limp hand, hanging down as he was carried.

"Doctor Berkley? Can you hear me? Are you alive? Oh, please, let him be alive," she gasped.

"He's very weak, but he's still alive," one of the men said, and they laid the doctor down on the sand, where Grace cradled his head in her hands.

His lips were blue, his face pale, and he was soaked through, covered in sand. Grace pulled out her handkerchief, dabbing at his brow, and now he opened his eyes, blinking against the brightness of the morning light.

"Grace..." he stammered.

"I'm here. I can hear you," she said, gently stroking his head.

"I... the wreck? The sailors?" he said, spluttering as he spoke.

"Some were rescued, others less fortunate. We need to get back to the cottage," she said, looking up at the rescuers, who now stooped down to lift the doctor from the sand.

But as they did so, he clasped at Grace's hand, groaning as he tried to speak.

"No, Grace. It's too late. You... you always made me proud. You'll make a fine physician. But now..." he gasped, and his lead lolled to one side.

Grace let out a cry, clasping at his hand, but it was no use. Doctor Berkley was dead, and now his body was brought to join the others on the harbour wall, where the curate had arrived to say prayers.

"O most powerful and glorious Lord God, at whose command the winds blow, and lift up the waves of the sea, and who stillest the rage thereof; We thy creatures, but miserable sinners, do in this our great distress cry unto thee for help; Save, Lord, or else we perish. We confess, when we have been safe, and seen all things quiet about us..." he was saying, reading from the prayer book.

But Grace was not listening. She stared at the lifeless bodies of the sailors, and at that of Doctor Berkley, too. He had been her dearest friend, her guardian, her family. Her mother was gone, Lady Edith was gone, and now Doctor Berkley was gone, too.

"A brave man," the landlord said, shaking his head as the curate concluded the prayers.

The small crowd of villagers dispersed, whilst a far larger

crown remained gather on the beach, hunting amidst the wreckage of the ship for whatever bounty remained. It was a sickening sight with a complete and utter disregard for life. Grace turned to find Captain Dickinson and Mrs. Parks watching her.

"And what happens to you now, Grace? You can't keep playing at nurses without a doctor to keep you company," Mrs. Parks said, smirking at Grace, who would gladly have seen the housekeeper perish in the wreck she had caused.

"They'll appoint a new doctor, and I doubt he'll want a nurse at his side. An interfering little fool, that's what you are, Grace," Captain Dickinson said, shaking his head.

"And you're both nothing but murderers," Grace retorted.

Mrs. Parks looked at her in surprise.

"You watch your tongue, Grace. Remember who you're speaking to," she snarled.

"Yes, the woman who wanted to poison Lady Edith, and who conspired to wreck the ship on the rocks. I know you did it, Mrs. Parks. I know you did it all, and not just you, all of them," Grace retorted.

She could hardly control the anger welling up inside her. Captain Dickinson stepped hurriedly forward, seizing Grace by the shoulders.

"You forget everything you just said. If you want to see the money you stole from my cousin, forget the rest. Do you understand?" he said, his voice low and menacing.

Grace met his gaze, defiant, even as she knew she had no evidence of what any of them had done. But in her heart, Grace knew the truth. She had heard enough to know it, and now she pulled away, turning her back on them, as tears rolled down her cheeks.

"You'll have to leave, Carshalton, Grace. You won't be able to stay here," Mrs. Parks called out, as Grace walked away.

She returned to the cottage in an exhausted state, throwing

herself down in a chair by the hearth and sobbing. The cottage, with its medical instruments and shelves of ointments and tonics, felt empty, and Grace no longer felt as though it was her home.

Doctor Berkley was gone, and Grace knew Mrs. Parks and Captain Dickinson were right – whoever replaced the doctor would not take kindly to the presence of a young girl, however much she had proved herself already.

"Everything always gets taken away," she told herself, as she sat in despair by the empty hearth.

A rumble of thunder echoed outside, and fresh storm clouds were gathering. The wreck would be swept out to sea, and it would be as though nothing had happened on that fateful night. Grace sighed, running her hands through her hair, and lamenting the tragic loss of the man she had come to love as her father. She thought about his last words, a weak smile coming over her face as she recalled what he had said.

"You made me proud... you'll make a fine physician," he had said, and it was to these words Grace clung.

"I'll make you proud, Doctor Berkley, I promise you," she said, uttering the words out loud, with a defiant tone, even as felt terrified for the future.

A low rumble of thunder echoed outside, and the pitter patter of rain now fell against the window. Grace shuddered to think of another ship wrecked on the rocks, and vowed to do all she could to put a stop to the wicked practice, even if it meant endangering her own life to do so.

"They know, I know, but I won't let them get away with. Not again," she said to herself, listening as another rumble of thunder echoed across the ravine, and the waves crashed on the rocks.

* * *

DOCTOR BERKLEY'S funeral had been a simple one, attended by only a handful of villagers. There were notable absences–Mrs. Wicks, the Langfords, and the curate's sister, all of whom found their excuses.

Captain Dickinson did not attend, either, nor did any of the servants from Carshalton House. Grace now knew who it was who had wrecked the ship–those who had not attended the funeral. It was chilling to think how many of the villagers profited from the wreckage, and she was certain even the curate had a hand in it, even as it was he who conducted the service.

"... come, ye blessed children of my Father, receive the kingdom prepared for you from the beginning of the world: Grant this, we beseech thee, O merciful Father, through Jesus Christ, our Mediator and Redeemer. Amen," the curate said, concluding the prayers of the burial.

The congregation said the grace together, and the mourners now dispersed, as Grace stood at the graveside. She had thrown a handful of dirt into it, as was custom, and now she watched as the gravedigger hurried forward to begin filling it in. A simple cross had been erected, and a brass plaque bore the doctor's name. He was only thirty-five years old.

"A good man," a voice behind Grace said, and she turned to find the landlord with his cap in hand, shaking his head.

He was dressed in an ill-fitting black mourning suit, and was sweating profusely in the sunshine of that warm day. He ran his finger around the edge of his drooping collar, sighing, as he gazed down at the rapidly filling grave.

"He was, yes. Thank you for trying to help him," Grace said, for she knew the landlord and other rescuers had done all they could.

"We wouldn't have had to if it wasn't for... well, you know," he said, and Grace nodded.

The wrecking had divided the village, and there were some who had accused others openly of being part of it. No one could say for certain who had flashed the light or who had been the first to take the spoils of the wreck, but many of the villagers had profited from it.

When the naval authorities had arrived to investigate, they had found the ship stripped of its cargo, and most of it washed back out to sea.

The sailors had been buried elsewhere, and Doctor Berkley's funeral marked the end of the matter, at least in the eyes of many.

"I know, and it can't be allowed to happen again," she said, shaking her head.

"I agree, but there're many in this village who wouldn't. Not least up at Carshalton House. But what can I do? What can any of us do? We bury the dead, we lament the loss, and wait for the next storm to come. They'll be waiting, too," the landlord said, and shaking his head, he went off muttering to himself, leaving Grace standing by the graveside.

On such a beautiful day, it was hard to believe the wickedness enacted out at sea. The waters were calm, and only the occasional plume of white spray broke the deep blue surface.

Far out on the horizon, Grace could just make out a ship, sailing a good distance from the rocks, and she shook her head, wondering how long it would be before another ship sank to its doom. The gravedigger had finished filling in the grave, and he went off whistling to himself, as Grace followed slowly behind.

Before she left the churchyard, she paused at her mother's grave, kneeling in front of the stone and putting her hand out to touch it.

"Let the dead bury the dead, that's what it says in the Bible, but everyone I love is here. You, Lady Edith, and now Doctor Berkley. How can I stay away?" she said out loud, tracing her fingers over the letters on her mother's headstone as a tear rolled down her cheek.

Grace would gladly have stayed in the churchyard forever,

lying down amidst the gently blowing wildflowers and falling asleep, never to reawaken. She stayed there until dusk, sitting by her mother's grave, and whispering her fears.

She was afraid of being sent away, and she felt certain the arrival of a new doctor would mean her life in Carshalton was over. She would be sent to an orphanage or the poorhouse, and she would certainly never see anything of Lady Edith's money.

'I've got no one now,' she told herself as she made her way back to the cottage.

It had been her home, but it belonged to the hospital board in Norwich, and with the death of Doctor Berkley, the appointment of a new doctor was already in process. It was the curate who had told her this, adopting a patronising tone as he had explained the process of Grace's departure.

"You'll be allowed to stay there in the meantime, though it's hardly right for a child to reside alone," he had said, but in this, Grace had been fortunate.

Doctor Berkley had been shrewd in making arrangements, and he had left her a small amount of money, should the worst happen. He had also stipulated a clause in the administration of the cottage attached to the role of doctor in Carshalton.

It came with a maid, and it would be up to the next doctor to make arrangements for said maid if her services were not required. Grace was to be this maid, even as Doctor Berkley had never treated her as such, or expected her to perform the duties she was now tasked with.

"It was Doctor Berkley's wish I be allowed to stay," Grace had replied, and the curate looked at her with a stern expression.

"You'll not find yourself welcome in Carshalton, Grace. Not any longer," he had said, narrowing his eyes in a threatening manner.

Grace had faced him defiantly. She knew the curate was part of the plot, just like so many others. It was said the rectory was amply supplied with brandy and cigars, even as the living itself was hardly a plumb one.

"I don't wish to be made welcome. The only people I care about are buried in the churchyard. I'd sooner join them than be made welcome. But I know what happened, and it's a wicked thing for anyone to be involved in," Grace had said, and she and the curate had parted ways on less than amicable terms.

Now, as she looked around the cottage, her once familiar home seemed a different place altogether. It was still filled with Doctor Berkley's things—his clothes, his books, his ornaments, his certificates, and the stern portrait of his mother and father on the wall.

Everything was familiar, and yet it would soon be taken away, and replaced by the personality of the doctor who next arrived to tend to the people of Carshalton. Doctor Berkley would be forgotten, even as Grace vowed to remember him.

She thought about her mother and Lady Edith. Soon, they, too, would only have Grace to remember them, and whilst she remained in a state of abject sorrow over the death of Doctor Berkley, there was comfort, at least, in knowing his memory lived on through her.

"I suppose I'd better get started. It'll only be a matter of days before the next doctor arrives," she said to herself, rolling up her sleeves, and determining to keep busy in the meantime—eager to prove her use to the new doctor, even as housekeeping was far from what she knew.

THE NEW DOCTOR

*G*race sneezed. She had been dusting the top of the Welsh dresser, and a cloud of dust had emanated from behind a display of Spode, the plates surely not having been touched in years.

"Goodness me, look at all this dust," she exclaimed, stifling another sneeze, and almost toppling from her step ladder.

She reached out warily with her feather duster, knowing it was only a matter of time before another cloud of dust arose from the upper crevices and corners of the cottage.

It was a week since Doctor Berkley's funeral, and Grace had kept herself busy by readying the cottage for the arrival of the new doctor. His name was Doctor Mullen, and she knew nothing more about him but that. He was due to arrive that day, travelling from London by train to Norwich and onto Carshalton by carriage.

It was the curate who had informed her of his arrival, reminding her again of her precarious position.

"I doubt he'll need a maid, whatever Doctor Berkley might've thought," he had said, but Grace remained defiant.

She was not about to be sent away, and if she was, she would have the money Doctor Berkley left her as compensation. She had made the cottage ready, and the only reminder of Doctor Berkley on show was his long, tubular stethoscope, a recent invention from France. It was engraved with his name, a present on the day of his taking the Hippocratic oath and stood upright in the corner of the parlour, where Doctor Berkley had conducted many of his consultations.

"I wonder what he'll be like—the new doctor?" Grace thought to herself, as now she finished the last of the dusting, and looked around her with a sigh.

The house was ready, but Grace was far from so. Her short life had known many changes—the death of her mother, the death of Lady Edith, the death of Doctor Berkeley, and now the arrival of a new doctor, one whom she knew nothing about.

"And what happens if he does send me away? What am I to do then? Where will go? I know nothing other than Carshalton," she told herself, shaking her head at the thought of what might become of her.

But she was soon drawn out of her thoughts by the sound of a horse and trap outside. The road down to the village was difficult to navigate for all but the most experienced carriage driver, and it was often the case that visitors took a horse and trap, driven by a farmhand, from the top of the hill into the village.

Grace hurried to the window, and she saw this very scene before her—the horse and trap belonging to Mr. Sykes at Brentwood Farm, and riding in the back of it, an elderly gentleman, with a crop of white hair, a ruddy face, and a pair of pince-nez spectacles perched on his nose.

Grace was surprised to see an elderly man. She had expected someone younger, like Doctor Berkley. But she was even more surprised to see a boy, perhaps the same age as her, sitting next to him.

"Here we are, Doctor Mullen, this is the cottage," the farmhand said, as he brought the horse to a halt at the end of the garden path.

Grace's heart was beating fast. She was unsure whether the doctor even knew she would be there, and now she watched as the boy jumped down from the trap to take the bags.

"What a beautiful place, Father," he said, and Grace gasped.

She had not expected the arrival of anyone else, let alone a boy of her own age, and now she went tentatively to the door, knowing she could not delay the inevitable any longer. As she opened it, both the doctor and his son looked up in surprise.

"Oh, are you sure this is the right place?" the doctor asked, calling back to the farmhand, who was now turning the horse.

"That's right, Doctor Mullen, that's just Grace. She lives with the doctor. At least she did," he said, shrugging his shoulders, as he led the horse away.

Doctor Mullen scratched his head, and the boy looked curiously at Grace. He had blonde hair, and bright blue eyes, with a keen face and the suggestion of an athletic build in the future. Grace blushed.

"Good afternoon, sir," she said, stepping back and holding the door open.

"But I think there's been some mistake. I wasn't expecting anyone. Who are you?" the doctor asked.

Grace was unsure how to introduce herself. She was the maid, and yet, with Doctor Berkley, she had been anything but a maid. She had been his nursing assistant, his friend, his companion, a daughter to him, and he, a father to her. They had never exchanged a cross word, and he had always encouraged her–albeit with a reminder of the difficulties involved–to pursue that which she dreamed of, to become a nurse like her mother before her.

"I'm... Grace," she stammered, and the doctor scratched his head again.

"Yes, but... why are you here? This is the doctor's cottage, isn't it? Goodness me, they told me Carshalton was a strange place, but... are you the maid?" he asked, as he made his way up the path, followed by the boy, who was dragging a large trunk behind him.

"I lived with Doctor Berkley. He was teaching me to be a nurse. I learned so much from him. I came here when my guardian, Lady Edith, died. Doctor Berkley took me in. I'm to be your maid, yes," Grace said.

The doctor shook his head.

"Really? I don't think this is going to work. I don't need a maid, and as for learning to be a nurse... well, you're only a child," he said, looking at Grace in disbelief.

"But I know so much," Grace replied, as she stepped back to allow the doctor to enter the cottage.

He looked around him with a critical eye, nodding, as his eyes rested on the medicine cabinet.

"Everything looks in order. Doctor Berkley's death was a tragedy, one I was sorry to hear about. He was a good man, by all accounts, and he's certainly left behind an ordered consulting room," Doctor Mullen said.

"Please, sir, it was me who ordered it. I know where every-thing goes, and how to order the medicines. I can show you," Grace said, going to the medicine cabinet and showing the doctor the system by which she and Doctor Berkley kept account of the medicines stored there.

Doctor Mullen nodded.

"Yes, well... that's all very well and good, but... this is a small cottage. It's hardly big enough for us all," he said,

"I sleep in the attic," Grace said, though Doctor Berkley had always insisted on her taking the second bedroom.

The cottage was not large, but it had always suited their purposes, and Grace was certain they could make things work. She did not want to be sent away, even as Doctor Mullen appeared in two minds as to the possibility. But to her surprise, it was the boy who now spoke up in her defence.

"Father, don't you think we should accept the situation as we find it, at least, for now? I think it's rather nice to find the cottage clean and tidy, the beds made, and the obvious skill of Doctor Berkley's assistant demonstrated," he said.

His father looked at him and smiled.

"Is that so? Well... yes, I suppose... it's not what I was expecting, but then... I didn't really know what to expect. Tell me... oh, I don't know your name," he said, looking somewhat embarrassed.

"Grace, Grace Carruthers," she said, and the doctor nodded.

"Well, Grace, You know my name, Doctor Mullen, Doctor Christopher Mullen, and this is my son, Thomas. He's away at boarding school for part of the year and serves as my assistant for the rest. But you say you were Doctor Berkley's assistant. Does that mean you furnish me with an account of the district, and of my patients?" he asked.

Grace *could* provide such an account. She knew everyone in Carshalton, and what was wrong with them, if anything, and what they believed was wrong with them, even in error. She knew Miss Byrne was a hypochondriac, and that Mr. McMahon's gout was always inflamed on a Monday after he had drunk a bottle of claret with his Sunday luncheon.

She knew Arthur Tooth was given over to believing himself the subject of numerous tropical diseases he read about in obscure journals, and that Lucy Berks regularly applied leeches to her skin for the apparent benefits of her health.

She knew all this, because Doctor Berkley had known it, and she had accompanied him wherever she went.

"I can, yes. And I've made something for you both to eat. You've had a long journey, and you should rest," she said.

The doctor's expression softened, and he nodded.

"That's very kind of you, I'm sure. Perhaps you could give me your account whilst we eat?" he said, and Grace nodded.

For now, it seemed, she was accepted, and having served the meal–a dish of mackerel, fresh from the return of the fishermen that morning–she set about telling Doctor Mullen everything she knew about Carshalton and its inhabitants.

* * *

"AND ALL THIS business of the wrecked ships–these waters are notorious, aren't they? Doctor Berkley perished in the rescue attempt," Doctor Mullen said, as Grace cleared away the plates.

"That's right. The rocks beneath the surface go far out to sea. These are shallow waters, and impossible to navigate unless you know precisely how to do so. Most ships sail wide of the ravine, but not all do," Grace replied.

She did not know whether to tell Doctor Mullen about the wreckers or not. The threats of Captain Dickinson, Mrs. Parks, the curate, and all the others weighed heavily on her mind, and Grace knew it could be dangerous to seek the doctor's support in the matter, even as she knew she was in the right.

There was no doubt in Grace's mind as to the guilt of those involved. The wrecking had been planned, and those responsible had waited for the right moment to strike. A violent storm, and the approach of a heavily laden cargo ship. They would watch and wait again. Of that, she was certain.

"What a truly terrible way to perish. One can only imagine the suffering of those poor men. And for Doctor Berkley to go to their rescue–a brave man. I hope the village recognises that," Doctor Mullen said.

"I'm sure they do," Grace replied, even as she knew better.

There were few in the village who had extolled him for what he had done. The curate had mentioned it only in passing during the eulogy at his funeral, and there had been no public recognition of his bravery.

It was as though the village thought his actions to be an inconvenience, rather than a cause for a memorial. Doctor Berkley had interfered, and the people of Carshalton did not care for interference.

"It's certainly a curious place. I'm looking forward to getting to know the people. But tell me, Grace, you followed Doctor Berkley, you learned from him. Did he really agree to teach you?" Doctor Mullen asked.

It seemed the physician had trouble understanding Grace's role, even as she nodded.

"He did. I can set a broken leg without assistance, and I know what all the medicines in the medicine cabinet do. I can recognise the symptoms of most common diseases, and I know the treatments, both scientific and herbal, though Doctor Berkley was trying to cure the residents of Carshalton of super-stition," Grace said, remembering some of the folk tales the villagers still believed, despite so many medical advancements.

Doctor Berkley had once spent over an hour trying to dissuade a young farm hand from driving a nail into his tooth, believing he could then drive the nail into a tree and transfer his pain there. The farm hand had been persuaded and Doctor Berkley had extracted the tooth with great care.

"Yes, I fear there'd still be a lingering sense of superstition in a place like this. I'm used to London, and the advancements of modernity," Doctor Mullen replied.

Grace was curious as to why he and Thomas had left behind the metropolis for an obscure backwater in Norfolk, and as she and Thomas washed the plates late that evening, she plucked up the courage to ask. Thomas seemed an amiable sort of person, and had shown no sign of looking down on Grace, offering to help her, even as she had insisted she could manage.

"What brought your father to Norfolk?" she asked.

Thomas smiled.

"He wants to... experience another side to medicine. He's spent much of his working life in hospitals. He's a marvellous surgeon and anatomist. And he knows about the mind, too. He's made studies in every field of medicine, but he doesn't feel as though he's ever put all his learning into practice. In a place like this, he might be setting a broken leg one moment, and dealing with a person who believe they're the King of England the next. That's what he wants," Thomas replied, and Grace nodded.

She could understand Doctor Mullen's desire to treat patients as they were in a place like Carshalton. Doctor Berkley had often spoken in similar terms. He had wanted to make a difference to the lives of those he treated and had come to Carshalton with bright eyed enthusiasm for the task ahead. But that did not mean there were not times when he found his patients trying.

The people of Carshalton could be difficult, and many of them were stubborn in refusing treatment or believing they knew best. The incident with the farmhand and the nail proved that.

"And that's what he'll get. It's a strange place," Grace replied, even as she had known no other.

But Grace had always felt something of an outsider in Carshalton, never entirely certain of her place there, and whilst she had nowhere else to go, she no longer felt as though she truly belonged, either.

"And what about you? Why did you end up living with Doctor Berkley? And why do you want to be a nurse? It's hardly a respected position, even though it should be," Thomas said.

Grace smiled. She knew nurses were looked down on, but she had also seen the way in which Lady Edith had come to depend on her mother. Grace's mother had been diligent in her ministrations and unfailingly dedicated to her work. Grace wanted to be like her, and she could think of nothing she would rather do than to nurse. It was in her blood, and now she explained something of her story to Thomas as they finished washing the dishes.

"And that's how I came to live with Doctor Berkley, but I don't miss Carshalton House. I hated it there–apart from being with Lady Edith, and before her, my mother. They made it bearable. But the servants are wicked, and I always dreaded going back there with Doctor Berkley," Grace said, shuddering at the thought of her encounters with Mrs. Parks since the day she had come to live at the doctor's cottage.

Thomas looked at her curiously, and Grace realised just how forceful her words must seem to an outsider. Thomas and his father knew nothing of the intrigues at Carshalton House, or of what Mrs. Parks and the other servants had done.

Even Captain Dickinson was involved, and it made Grace shudder to think of what might occur when another storm blew up and another ship was sighted by the ever-vigilant Mrs. Wicks.

"It sounds like a horrible place. I'm glad I'll be returning to boarding school soon," Thomas said.

At that moment, Doctor Mullen appeared at the kitchen door. He was holding Doctor Berkley's stethoscope, holding it up with an evident look of pleasure.

"I see it's got his name engraved on it. Would he mind me using it, do you think? It's a fine instrument," he said, and Grace shook her head.

"He'd be glad to think it was being used, I'm sure," she replied, and Doctor Mullen smiled.

"I'm sorry for my initial surprise at your presence, Grace. I simply wasn't expecting anyone to be here to help me. That's why I brought Thomas. Will you accompany me on my first round tomorrow? You can both come, and you can tell us everything about the patients they won't tell us themselves," he said, and Grace smiled.

"I'd be pleased to," Grace replied, glancing at Thomas, who smiled.

"Father can be quite a stickler for precision," he said, and Doctor Mullen raised his eyebrows.

"Is that so, Thomas?" he replied, and Thomas fell silent.

But Grace was only too happy at the thought of accompanying the new doctor on his rounds, and she felt certain she could prove herself to him with her knowledge of medicine and all she had learned from Doctor Berkley.

"I'd be happy to," she said, and Doctor Mullen smiled.

"Then it seems I'm to have a nurse, as well as doctor in training," he replied.

THE WRECKERS' WARNING

"$\mathcal{M}$rs. Wilks isn't entirely trustworthy when it comes to reporting her own condition," Grace said, as she, Doctor Mullen, and Thomas left the elderly lady's cottage the next morning.

Doctor Mullen smiled.

"Yes, I think she could do a lot more for herself, and I noticed she hadn't been taking any of the medication Doctor Berkley prescribed for her. What was it she said? It's just the "quack's potion." Well, it's been a long time since I've been called a quack," Doctor Mullen said.

As they had gone about their rounds that morning, Grace had begun to realise just how eminent a doctor, the new physician in Carshalton was. He was certainly no quack, but had published groundbreaking studies in numerous fields, and was an expert in everything from physiology to disorders of the mind.

He had told Grace of his desire to make a study of an ordinary parish, with all its varied forms of disease and ailment, and that he intended to write up his findings in a book.

"She always called Doctor Berkley a quack. But she knows a

lot more than she lets on. There's not much in Carshalton she doesn't know about," Grace replied.

She had noticed the lamp by the window in Mrs. Wilks' bedroom, and remembered Doctor Berkley's words about the old women being a principal lookout for incoming ships on stormy days.

"Is that so? Well, she didn't take kindly to my suggestions. I don't understand why people won't take sound medical advice. So many still prefer charms and amulets to proper medical evidence," Doctor Mullen said, tutting and shaking his head.

They were walking down Howard's Hill, in the direction of the village, their rounds concluded for the morning. Grace had explained each case with the methodical approach Doctor Berkley had taught her, outlining the condition, stating the facts as known, and advising as to the current treatment.

There was nothing Doctor Mullen had not agreed on, though he had been able to make some additional suggestions in several cases, all of which had been to the benefit of the patients involved.

"I'm astonished at all the things you know," Thomas said as they came to the cottage a short while later.

"I just... well, I always listened to Doctor Berkley. He always explained things to me, and not in a patronising way. He stated the facts, and that's how I learned," Grace replied.

She had never thought of it as astonishing. Doctor Berkley had taught her, and she had learned. That was that.

"Yes, but you understand it, too. That's what's so remarkable. You recall each case, you know the treatment, and you can make diagnoses. I want to be a doctor, like my father, but I know nothing compared to you," Thomas said, and it seemed he was in genuine awe of Grace, who saw herself as nothing more than the doctor's assistant.

They ate a simple luncheon of bread and cheese before Doctor Mullen sat down at his desk to deal with his correspondence. He and Thomas's things were being sent from London, and the cottage remained somewhat spartan in its decoration and character. Doctor Berkley's things having been packed away into the attic, where Grace had spent the night. She did not mind sleeping there, and had pulled her bed close to the window, allowing her to look out to see and watch the waves crashing on the rocks.

"I'll help you with the dishes," Thomas said, and he and Grace cleared the plates from the table.

Grace had just drawn water from the well at the back of the cottage, when the sound of horse's hooves caused her to look up. To her surprise, Captain Dickinson had just ridden up to the cottage gate and was dismounting from his horse.

He did not notice Grace, who was watching him from the garden to the side of the cottage, and now he made his way up the path, knocking loudly at the door. Grace hurried back inside to answer it, but Doctor Mullen had already done so and was ushering his visitor inside. Thomas looked at Grace curiously.

"Who is it?" he whispered as Grace closed the kitchen the door, leaving a slight gap to hear something of the conversation.

"It's Captain Dickinson. He's Lady Edith's heir. It was him who threw me out of the house, and him who denies me my inheritance," Grace replied, for she had explained her relationship to Lady Edith the previous evening, and Thomas was well aware of the captain's shortcomings.

He nodded, and the two of them listened at the door. It was not difficult to overhear the conversation. Captain Dickinson had a loud, booming voice, and he was addressing Doctor Mullen in an overbearing and dictatorial manner.

"I own most of the village, and most of the land surrounding it, too," he was saying, and Grace made a face.

"He only likes to think he does," she whispered, as Doctor Mullen now replied.

"I see, and am I to have some special care for Carshalton House?" he asked.

"You're to have a care for the whole village, Doctor Mullen, but you'll soon find there're elements in Carshalton of an unwelcome nature. Troublemakers," Captain Dickinson replied.

Grace made a face. She knew Captain Dickinson was referring to her and trying to win the doctor over to his side. She could only hope Doctor Mullen was wise enough to see it.

"So far, I've only found a case of gout, a sprained ankle, and the measles," Doctor Mullen said.

"With the greatest of respect, Doctor Mullen, you've only been here a day or so. I wanted to call on you in the hope of impressing on you the foolishness of certain ideas pertaining to recent events in the village," Captain Dickinson continued.

Grace knew what was coming. Lady Edith's heir would now attempt to make it seem as though the wreck had been a terrible accident, a tragedy, and not the fault of the wreckers. Doctor Berkley had come close to spoiling his and the other's ambitions, even as he had paid for it with his life. But Doctor Mullen was a man of conviction, and Grace felt certain he could not be easily fooled. She glanced at Thomas, who was listening intently at her side.

"And what events might they be?" Doctor Mullen replied.

"You'll have heard about the shipwreck? How couldn't you have done, given it was your predecessor's downfall? There're those who think the shipwreck was caused by wreckers. But that's nonsense. The rocks are notoriously hard to navigate, even for the most able captain. A storm blew up, the ship was wrecked, and any rumour to the contrary can't be allowed to take hold," Captain Dickinson said.

Grace shook her head.

"It's not true," she whispered, hoping Doctor Mullen would not be so easily swayed.

"I don't know about wreckers and shipwrecks, but I know a

good deal of the cargo was stolen from the hull of the ship the following day. The magistrate told me as much when I called on him for a report of the parish whilst in Norwich. It would make me shudder to think anyone was capable of such a thing," Doctor Mullen replied.

"There's no law against taking things washed up on a beach. How can they be proved to belong to anyone? No, doctor, the sinking of the ship was a terrible accident. Any suggestion to the contrary would be unwise. You'll hear rumours, of course– not least from the child who resides under your roof, but don't listen to them," Captain Dickinson said.

Grace's heart skipped a beat. She had not told Doctor Mullen, or Thomas, of her suspicions surrounding the wreckers. She was certain Captain Dickinson was at the heart of it all, even as she had no way of proving so. Now, she stared at Thomas, who furrowed his brow, even as Doctor Mullen now laughed.

"Really, Captain Dickinson. She's only a child. What could she possibly know about such things? I'm here to do a job. I'm a doctor, and I'm not about to get mixed up in village gossip. I'm sure the rocks can be very dangerous, and I'm sure many ships have met their fate there," he said.

"That's right, Doctor Mullen," the captain replied, but the doctor now continued.

"Just as I know human nature well enough to see advantages taken when opportunities arise. A wrecked ship brings with it the possibility of gain, whilst coaxing a ship to its doom does the same. There may be wreckers along this coast, there may not, but I intend to carry out my duties with diligence, and be a faithful physician to all who come to me for help," he said.

Grace was relieved, even as she knew Captain Dickinson would not take kindly to such words.

"Be careful, doctor. I warn you again. Don't listen to

rumours! Good day to you," Captain Dickinson replied, and the doctor bid him farewell.

Grace watched from the kitchen window as Lady Edith's heir strode down the garden path. His face was set with anger, and he treated his horse roughly as he rode away.

"What a horrible man," Thomas said, and Grace turned back from the window.

She was about to answer when a summons came from the parlour and Doctor Mullen called them both into his company.

"I'm sure you can't have failed to overhear the conversation with Captain Dickinson. He spoke disparagingly of you, Grace. But I want to hear your version of events. Do you believe there're wreckers along this coast?" he asked, and Grace nodded.

"I do, sir," she replied, and she went on to tell the doctor and Thomas everything she knew and everything she suspected.

She told them about Doctor Berkley's concerns, and the brave manner in which he had attempted to thwart the wreckers' plans, and she told them of her suspicions against the captain and the other servants at Carshalton House.

"And you actually overheard the housekeeper speaking of such things?" Doctor Mullen said, shaking his head in astonishment.

"I did, sir, yes. She was speaking with one of the gardeners. His name's Dolby. But it's not just them, Doctor Mullen. It's the whole village–Mrs. Wicks with her lamp to signal the arrival of ships off the coast, the curate with his pious prayers for the survivors, the Langfords, with their barns full of the haul from the ships. Everyone's in on it," Grace said, knowing the enormity of what she was saying, and what she was accusing so many of being involved in.

Doctor Mullen furrowed his brow.

"It's a remarkable story, and perhaps I'd find it too incredible to believe, but I've heard rumours of something like this. The wild and lonely Norfolk coastline, the storms blowing up, the wrecked ships. They call the passage through the seas here the Devil's Way, and for good reason, it seems. No, Grace, I believe you. And I certainly don't trust Captain Dickinson, lauding it over me like that. Who does he think he is?" he said, and Grace gave a sigh of relief.

She had feared Doctor Mullen would side with Captain Dickinson against her, that he would send her away for making such wild accusations. For how could anyone suspect a clergyman of being involved in such wickedness? Or an invalided old lady? But that was the point. That had always been the point.

Carshalton appeared like any other English village, with its church and inn, its farms and cottages, its big house, and a cast of genteel characters. But underneath, there lay a wickedness, one in which almost all the village was involved.

"I'm glad you believe me, Doctor Mullen. Doctor Berkley was so brave. He stood up to them, and yet, he paid for it with his life," Grace said.

Doctor Berkley had paid for his bravery with his life, and those responsible for the wrecking had blood on their hands. Grace knew she could never rest until those responsible were brought to justice, and until it was proved what had been happening in the village and with the wreckers.

"I do believe you, Grace, but we must be careful. We've no proof as to anyone's involvement, and I understand the wreck is being blamed on poor navigation and the storm. I fear this won't be the last of the wrecks," Doctor Mullen said, shaking his head sadly.

"But we've got to do something, Father, we're sworn to save lives. Isn't that what Doctor Berkley did? He took his Hippocratic oath to the grave–do no harm, and prevent harm where we can," Thomas said.

His father nodded.

"You're right, Thomas, but we're bound by the law, too, and we need proof if we're to make such bold claims against so many. But as a physician, I'm in a unique situation. I'm invited into the home of any person in the village, if they're sick, that is, and if we bide our time, we can gather the evidence we need. I noticed that curious lamp by the bed in Mrs. Wicks' bedroom, and when I met the curate, I couldn't help but feel he lacked any sense of compassion for the survivors of the wreck. Little by little, that's how we'll discover the full extent of this wickedness. Don't worry, Grace, Doctor Berkley's death won't be in vain," he replied.

Later that day, Thomas asked Grace to walk with him on the headland. He wanted to see the place where the wreckers had stood, and Grace agreed to accompany him.

She liked Thomas. He was curious about the world around him, and entirely dedicated to pursuing his intention to become a doctor. They climbed up the steep path of the ravine, and onto the headland, where the path continued along the edge of a sandy bank, with the cliffs falling into the sea below.

On a day like this, when the weather was calm, and the sea gently cresting its waves, it was hard to imagine the scene of horror played out there on the night of the wreck.

"It makes me shudder to think of it. How could anyone stand here and flash a lamp to lure men to their deaths?" Thomas said, shaking his head.

They had come to the point on the headland where Grace assumed the wreckers had stood. A hollow in the sand bank provided the perfect place from which to signal, and Grace imagined Mrs. Parks and Dolby gleefully flashing their lamp.

She looked across to the far side of the ravine, to the woods, where she and Doctor Berkley had made their desperate attempt at signal and rescue. From her vantage point, and in the daylight, Grace could see the jagged line of rocks stretching out below the surface of the sea. The waves were breaking on them, just enough to be invisible from afar.

Any ship sailing towards a light shone from the headland was doomed. It would be grounded on the rocks, its hull split in two, just as had happened to the wrecked ship.

"Because they're wicked people. I've known some of them all my lives, and it doesn't surprise me one bit. But others... it's horrible to think of it, but... I'm so glad you believe me, and your father does, too," Grace said, as they sat in the hollow looking out to sea.

Thomas turned to her and nodded.

"Why wouldn't we believe you?" he asked, and Grace was grateful to have found someone in whom she could confide.

"I'm not used to being believed. Well... I mean, I've lost everyone I ever cared about. My mother, Lady Edith, Doctor Berkley–they're all gone, and I'm left with no one. I was worried in case... well, in case I'd be sent away," Grace replied, fighting back the tears in her eyes.

But Thomas shook his head.

"My father isn't like that. He always tries to help people. That's what it means to be a doctor. He'd never have sent you away. I know he was a little confused at first, but I promise you'll stay here," Thomas replied, smiling at Grace, who felt a sense of relief at hearing these words.

Her life had been so filled with uncertainty and the unhappiness of loss. She was grateful to Doctor Mullen, and Thomas, for believing her, and for allowing her to stay.

"I'm so glad to hear it. I feared... well, I've never known anything else but Carshalton, and to be sent away..." she said, shaking her head at the thought.

Thomas thought for a moment, looking curiously at Grace.

"What brought you here to Carshalton? Why did your mother come here?" he asked.

Grace was unsure. She knew so little about the first years of her life–where they had been spent, and why she and her mother had come to Carshalton in the first place.

"Well… I think it was because my mother was to be a nurse to Lady Edith. I don't know exactly when we came here, but I can't remember anything else but being here. My first memories are of sitting in front of the hearth in Lady's Edith's bedroom. I remember my mother telling me she'd put me down to play as she was tending to Lady Edith," Grace replied.

But still, Thomas looked at her curiously.

"But doesn't it seem odd–a nurse with a baby? Servants don't normally have children, do they? I'm surprised Lady Edith allowed your mother to have you there and still nurse her. Wouldn't she have been better off with a different nurse?" Thomas asked.

Grace had never considered this question before. But Thomas was right. It *was* unusual for a servant to have a child, even as Grace had never considered her growing up at Carshalton House to be anything other than normal.

Lady Edith had treated her as her own and taken her as her ward after her mother's death. Again, Grace had never thought anything odd about this, even as it surely appeared so to others.

"Well… yes, I suppose so, but… it does seem off, doesn't it? But I don't know why my mother was chosen, or why Lady Edith was so adamant I should be her ward. I'm grateful, of course, but… it does seem odd, doesn't it?" Grace replied, her mind now filled with doubts as to her childhood and her upbringing.

As they walked back along the headland, Grace continued to ponder these questions, distracted from Thomas's conversation, and feeling a sense of something missing. As they came to the churchyard, Grace made her excuses and remained there.

"I'll see you back at the cottage," Thomas called out, hurrying off along the path.

It was beginning to rain, but Grace hardly noticed, as she

hurried through the gate an across the churchyard to her mother's grave. The rain was becoming heavy, and she kneeled in front of the grave, reaching out to touch the lichen covered headstone.

"Who am I, Mother?" she asked, for it was a question she could not answer for herself.

AN EXTRAORDINARY TRUTH

*T*homas's questions continued to haunt Grace in the days to come, and she began to realise just how little she knew about her past, and about why her mother had brought her to Carshalton House. The identity of her father was a mystery, and Grace knew nothing of her mother's origins, save for a vague notion she had come from London.

"I wish I'd asked Lady Edith more about her," Grace thought to herself as she cleared away the evening meal that night, a week after she and Thomas had walked on the headland.

Doctor Mullen had now established his round, and he had returned late that evening, having attended a birth at one of the outlying farms.

"There's a storm coming. I was hurrying to get home before it broke," the doctor had said, entering the cottage, just as the pitter patter of rain began to fall against the windowpanes.

As they had eaten dinner, thunder had rumbled over the ravine, and the rain had grown harder, now a deluge. Thomas had retired to his bedroom to study, and Grace was washing the dishes when Doctor Mullen entered the kitchen, interrupting her thoughts.

"Oh, I'm sorry, Doctor Mullen," she said, looking up to find him standing in the doorway.

He smiled at her.

"It's all right. I've noticed you deep in thought these past few days. Is everything all right?" he asked as Grace put down the plate she was washing.

"It is, it's just... something Thomas said to me. He asked me about my mother, and I realised I really know nothing about her, and certainly not about my father. I wish I'd asked more questions," she said, and Doctor Mullen nodded.

"It's always the way. I never knew my father, either. I grew up in the poorhouse with my mother. We had nothing, but a kindly benefactor took pity on me, and I was given a scholarship to the local grammar school. I owe him everything, but I know nothing of my father," Doctor Mullen said, shaking his head.

"I just wish I'd asked more questions," Grace repeated, and Doctor Mullen smiled.

"It's a wonderful thing, hindsight. I'm sure your mother loved you very much. We don't always need to know any more about a person than that," he replied.

Grace was about to thank him, but a shout from upstairs caused them both to startle, and Thomas's footsteps now clattered on the stairs.

"Quickly, come and look. There's a light flashing on the headland," he called out.

Grace and Doctor Mullen hurried after him, and they climbed up to the attic, all three of them peering through the window towards the sea. It was dusk, and Thomas was right. A light was flashing on the headland, just as it had done on the night Doctor Berkley had died.

"They're trying to wreck a ship! There must be one out at sea. Come on, we'll head them off," Doctor Mullen said, and before either Grace or Thomas could protest, he had hurried back downstairs.

"It's too dangerous. If they're capable of wrecking a ship, they're capable of..." Grace said, fearing for Doctor Mullen's safety, as now she and Thomas followed him downstairs.

The rain was driving against the windows, and the thunder rumbling around the ravine. Doctor Mullen pulled on his coat and hat, and Grace and Thomas did the same, following him out into the gathering dusk, soaked to the skin immediately by the driving rain.

"This way," Grace called out, leading them towards the headland.

But as they came to the path, a flash of lightning lit up the sky, and for a moment, Grace could see out to sea. The waves were crashing against the rocks, and the water and surging and swelling. She could see a ship far out beyond the stretch of rocks. It was in full sail, and as another flash of lightning lit up the scene, she let out a cry of relief.

"Look, it's sailing on. It's not seen the light, or it's ignored it. They've sailed beyond the danger. The waters are far deeper there, they'll make it," she exclaimed, feeling a sense of utter relief, as Doctor Mullen and Thomas paused, looking back at her, as another flash of lightning illuminated the scene.

"Thank God," Doctor Mullen said, catching his breath.

But as he did so, Grace could hear voices on the wind, and she beckoned them both off the path, as the outline of several figures came into view along the headland. Grace, Doctor Mullen, and Thomas hid amongst the bushes, where the darkness protected them from being seen.

"We should've flashed earlier. They'd have seen us then," a voice was saying, and Grace realised with horror it was that of the housekeeper, Mrs. Parks.

"If we'd flashed earlier, they'd have known there was no

lighthouse to guide them. It wasn't yet dusk," another voice replied, and Grace recognised it as that of Captain Dickinson.

"Or perhaps they've begun to realise – oh, perhaps it's time to stop," another voice said.

"Be quiet, curate. You don't complain when you're drinking fine brandy after dinner, or smoking the finest pipe tobacco, do you? No... we were unlucky this time, but next time..." Captain Dickinson said, and Grace recoiled in horror as the shadowy figures passed by.

They waited several moments, hardly daring to breathe, before Doctor Mullen patted Grace's arm.

"I think it's safe now. My goodness. What wickedness. But now we know–there's no doubt about it. Those are the wreckers. It's too ghastly for words. They'd have brought the ship onto the rocks tonight, just as they did on the night Doctor Berkley died. Those poor men on the ship–only saved by the grace of God. Come now, let's go home," the doctor said, and he ushered Grace and Thomas from their hiding place.

As they entered the cottage a short while later, Grace hurried to light the lamps, as Doctor Mullen sat down at the parlour table with a sigh.

"I'll make us some cocoa," Thomas said, poking at the embers in the range with the poker, to coax the flames back to life.

Doctor Mullen shook his head and banged his fist down angrily on the table.

"A whole village gone mad. Greed, that's what it is. It's astonishing," he said, as Grace came to sit next to him.

"I knew it was them–and there's no doubt now," she said.

"Well... I can't sit idly by and allow it to continue. I don't have any proof of the matter. It's my word against theirs, and who's going to believe a country doctor over the Lord of the Manor and a clergyman? But I've got to tell them I know about what they're doing. I've got to make them see they can't continue with this wickedness," he exclaimed, running his hands through his hair, a look of anger on his face.

Thomas had set the kettle to boil, and it was not long before the cocoa was made and the three had dried off from the rain and warmed up. They sat up until late, discussing what had happened, and what they might do about it.

Grace was fearful, for she knew what Captain Dickinson was capable of, even as Doctor Mullen seemed determined to confront him.

"You must be careful," she said, but the Doctor's mind was made up, and after breakfast the next morning, the three of them set off for Carshalton House...

* * *

"HE'LL ONLY DENY IT," Grace said, as they made their way across the lawn from the path leading through the woodland down to the ravine.

Grace disliked coming to Carshalton House. It held too many memories for her and was a very different place than it had been under Lady Edith. The gardens were largely turned over to vegetables and gone were the pretty beds of flowers Lady Edith had always so delighted.

The house itself appeared cold and foreboding, with many of the windows shuttered, and no sense of anyone calling it a home. Doctor Mullen marched straight up to the main door, even as Grace had suggested they knock first at the side door leading to below stairs.

"No, I intend to see Captain Dickinson himself," Doctor Mullen replied, and he knocked loudly at the door.

A few moments later, it was opened by Mrs. Parks, who looked surprised to see the doctor accompanied by Grace and Thomas.

"Were you sent for, doctor?" she asked, as Doctor Mullen fixed her with a stern gaze.

"I wasn't, no, Mrs. Parks. But I've come to see Captain Dickinson. It's a matter of the utmost urgency," he replied.

The housekeeper looked surprised.

"I can't imagine what would be so urgent," she replied, but Doctor Mullen was insistent, and now Mrs. Parks stepped back, admitting them entry, even as she warned them Captain Dickinson would not take kindly to being disturbed.

"It's a chance I'll take, Mrs. Parks," Doctor Mullen replied, as the housekeeper led them through the house to the captain's study–once Lady Edith's music room.

The house had changed considerably since Grace had last been inside, and many of the paintings and portraits had been removed, along with the décor and furnishings favoured by Lady Edith.

It felt a foreboding place, and Grace would much rather have remained at the cottage, even as she had not wished to see the doctor face Captain Dickinson alone.

"What is it? Didn't I tell you I didn't want to be disturbed?" Captain Dickinson called out, as Mrs. Parks knocked at the door of his study.

"Doctor Mullen insists on seeing you, sir," the housekeeper replied.

The door was opened, and the angry face of the captain looked out at them.

"I suppose this isn't a house call, Doctor Mullen? Or are you intending to tell me I'm sick?" he asked.

"The sickness of a madman, perhaps, Captain Dickinson," Doctor Mullen replied, facing the captain defiantly, even as his face grew even redder with anger.

"What? What do you mean?" he exclaimed, as Doctor Mullen stepped forward.

"We'll talk about it in here," he replied, pushing past Captain

Dickinson, and entering the study, closely followed by Grace and Thomas.

The musical instruments were gone, replaced by weighty tomes and a large desk covered in papers. Mrs. Parks followed, closing the door behind her and leaning against it, as Captain Dickinson glared at Doctor Mullen, who had seated himself without invitation in a chair by the hearth.

"You dare to come here, to enter my house, to..." he began, but Doctor Mullen interrupted him.

"We know what you were doing last night–the two of you, the curate, and goodness knows who else. We saw you on the headland flashing your lamp to draw the ship out to sea onto the rocks. We know what you've been doing," Doctor Mullen said.

Captain Dickinson glanced at Mrs. Parks, the hint of a smile playing across his lips.

"Is that so, doctor? And what proof do you have of it? Are you accompanied by a magistrate? Did you catch me in the act?" he asked, sneering as Doctor Mullen faced him defiantly.

"We saw you returning from the headland. We heard you talking about your wicked scheme. We know what you were doing," Doctor Mullen replied, but Captain Dickinson waved his hand dismissively.

"You don't know anything. I admit to being on the headland last night. Mrs. Parks and I share an unusual hobby with the curate–moth collecting. Haven't you heard of moth collecting, Doctor Mullen? I'm surprised. You're a medical man, it must surely interest you. Moths, as I'm sure you know, come out at night, and they're attracted to lamp light. What most people don't realise is just how fortunate we are in our moth species here in Norfolk. The headland is a noted area for their study. What you thought to be lamp flashing to wreck a ship was merely myself and my fellow enthusiasts collecting moths. Sadly, it was a disappointing night," he said, his eyes narrowing, and fixing Doctor Mullen with an angry glare.

"What nonsense," Doctor Mullen thundered, rising from his chair and pointing angrily at Captain Dickinson, who began to laugh.

"Nonsense, is it? Prove it," he snarled.

"We all heard you–all three of us. And I've overheard you, too–you and Dolby," Grace said, pointing at Mrs. Parks, who had been standing silently by the door.

The housekeeper's eyes narrowed.

"Are you threatening me, Grace?" she asked.

"We know what you've been doing. You're all in on it," Doctor Mullen said.

"And we won't rest until we prove it. It's been going on for years. Doctor Berkley knew about it, and he paid for it with his life, but I'm not..." Grace exclaimed, fighting back the tears, even as Mrs. Parks now interrupted her.

"You think yourself so high and mighty, don't you, Grace? Like butter wouldn't melt," she said.

Grace faced her defiantly. She was not afraid of the housekeeper, or of Captain Dickinson, or any of them. She thought of her mother, and of how she had always taught Grace the value of life, just as Doctor Berkley had done the same.

"I know what's right, and I know what's wrong. This is wrong," Grace said, but at these words, the housekeeper's face broke into a smile.

"And where did you learn that from, Grace? Your mother?" she asked.

Grace nodded. She was emphatic about that. Her mother had taught her right from wrong. And she had embodied it in her own life, too. Grace had always taken her mother as an example, and she knew there was no one else she trusted more to provide that example.

"I did, and I'm proud of it. She'd be the first to stand up to you, and to tell you what you're doing is wicked," Grace replied, but Mrs. Parks shook her head, and to Grace's astonishment she laughed.

"Oh, but you don't understand, Grace. Your mother was the worst of us all. Didn't you ever wonder why you came to Carshalton House? Didn't you ever wonder why Lady Edith took you as her ward? It's quite simple, Grace. Your mother was a wrecker, just like us, and it was only when she discovered you in the wreckage of one of the ships, she had a change of heart... she's not even your mother," Mrs. Parks said, with a gleeful look on her face, as Grace stared at her in horror.

"No, it can't be... it isn't," she stammered, as Captain Dickinson, too, began to laugh.

"And it only gets better, Grace. Your dear, darling Lady Edith, well, she wasn't what you thought her to be. She was one, too—a wrecker like the rest. I hope you see it now, Doctor Mullen, they were the real villains in all of this," he said, as tears rolled down Grace's cheeks.

It could not be true. She refused to believe it was true. Her mother could not have been a wrecker. She was a good and saintly woman who had always taught Grace the difference between right and wrong.

"No, I won't believe it. I can't believe it. It isn't true. My mother wasn't like that. You're lying," Grace cried out as Doctor Mullen stared in disbelief.

"She was—she came here from London to work for Lady Edith as her secretary, but soon learned more to her advantage. They were in on it together. Ships have been wrecked along this coast for hundreds of years. Lady Edith's father was infamous for it, though no one could ever prove it, of course. She carried on the tradition, and we servants had our share, too. But if you think you can prove it, you'll find the trail goes cold when your mother found you," Mrs. Parks said.

Grace shook her head. She was no foundling, adopted by the

woman she called mother. Her mother *was* her mother, and she had never told Grace any different.

"It's not true," Grace repeated, but Mrs. Parks shook her head.

"The ship was called *The Honoria*. It was Mrs. Wicks who sighted it that night. She flashed the light from the cottage, and Dolby saw it from the garden. Your mother and Lady Edith hurried to make preparations, but it was your mother who flashed the light. I'd go with her, and we'd watch from the headland, waiting for the right to moment signal. Your mother prided herself on knowing the tides and currents on this part of the coast, and she'd flash the lamp at just as the ship entered the Devil's Way. They had no chance, and the wreck was washed up on the shore. But the next morning, when your mother and I were taking our share, we heard the cry of a baby..." Mrs. Parks said.

Grace shook her head, trying not to be taken in by the words of the housekeeper, even as they answered so many of her questions.

"No... my father was... but I... it can't be," Grace stammered.

"It's true, you foolish child. We found you there. By a miracle, you'd survived the shipwreck. Your mother–Mary–brought you back here. Lady Edith didn't want to draw attention to the wreck. She feared it would arouse suspicion if we made your discovery known. Your mother decided to keep you, and that's when things changed," the housekeeper replied.

"But... how did they change?" Grace asked, even as she still could not bring herself to believe what Mrs. Parks was saying.

"Your adopted mother, as we should call her, realised the error of her ways. Lady Edith, too. They saw in you the lives lost, and that was the end of it. There was no more wrecking, and we were forbidden from speaking of it. But some of us didn't forget," she said, glancing at Captain Dickinson, who smiled.

"Hence my fascination with moth collecting," he replied.

Grace shook her head. She could not believe it, and now she looked at Doctor Mullen, who stepped forward and held out his hand to her.

"Come along, Grace. We're leaving," he said, as Mrs. Parks opened the study door, still with a smirk on her face.

"You know the truth now, Grace," she said, following them out into the hallway.

"We know the truth about a lot of things, Mrs. Parks — about you, and Captain Dickinson, and everyone involved in this wickedness," Doctor Mullen replied.

Captain Dickinson had followed them out into the hallway, and he laughed, pointing them to the door and gesturing for them to leave.

"And where's your proof, Doctor Mullen? I've got plenty of moths. Be gone with you, and unless you want the good name of Grace's apparent mother, and the even nobler name of Grace's benefactress dragged through the mud. Your own, too! I suggest you forget whatever it is you believe you know," he said, and with that, they were dismissed.

As they crossed the lawn towards the path leading through the woods into the ravine, Grace paused, glancing back towards the house, as Doctor Mullen put his hand on her shoulder.

"I don't know if it's true, Grace. Perhaps it is, and perhaps it isn't. But don't let those wicked words besmirch the memory of your mother, for she *was* your mother, whether by flesh and blood, or the bond of love. Remember her as you always have," Doctor Mullen said.

But Grace was struggling to do so. She had thought she knew all she needed to know about her mother–her kindness, her smile, her love. But all that was gone, replaced by the horrible thought of what she could be responsible for. And Lady Edith, too–the kind, gentle, loving soul who had given Grace a home when her mother had died.

"But I can't think of her like that now. Not after they've put such thoughts into my mind," Grace replied, and Doctor Mullen sighed.

"It's not easy discovering the truth, whatever that might be. But we can't just accept the word of Mrs. Parks and Captain Dickinson. We'll find the truth, Grace, I promise," he replied, and with a gentle hand, he led her away.

But as they passed the churchyard, Grace paused, gazing through the open gate towards the grave of her mother, and across to the monument in memory of Lady Edith.

"I don't believe them, I never did," she said to herself, and with this dreadful thought in her mind, Grace wondered if she would ever again find peace, knowing the dreadful things her mother had done. The very things she herself so abhorred.

PART III

A TRUTH-SEEKING HEART

Spring 1876

"There we are, Miss Lawson. Keep it elevated. If you put pressure on it, any pressure, it'll take longer to heal," Grace said, rising to her feet, as her patient looked up at her and smiled.

"Thank you, Grace. I don't know how I did it. Well... I just fell. I must be getting old," Miss Lawson said, and Grace smiled.

"Accidents happen, Miss Lawson. I'm glad I've been able to help," she said, as she picked up her roll of bandage and replaced her scissors in her medical bag.

Doctor Mullen had sent Grace to one of his easier house calls. Miss Lawson was a spinster who lived in a cottage by the harbour wall. She had sprained her ankle, and the grocery boy had come to the doctor's cottage to ask if Doctor Mullen might attend.

"She doesn't need a doctor. You go, Grace. You're more than capable," Doctor Mullen had said.

Grace was now eighteen years old, and there was little she did not know about the practicalities of medicine. For the past six years, she had been Doctor Mullen's assistant, just as she had been for Doctor Berkley before him.

Time and again, Grace had proved her skills more than worthy of acclaim, and was often sent out to deal with patients alone.

"Well, I'm glad it's you that came and not Doctor Mullen," Miss Lawson said, as Grace prepared to leave.

"Oh, it's not that he's too busy..." Grace began, but the patient shook her head.

"It's not that. It's just... well, his bedside manner leaves something to be desired. When I had that terrible stomach pain, he did nothing more than tell me to drink plenty of water and take those horrible salt tablets he prescribed," she said.

Grace smiled. Doctor Mullen could be brusque in his manner, but there was no doubting he had a physician's heart, and he had done much to care for the residents of Carshalton during his tenure as the village doctor. Alongside Grace, he had treated everything from measles and mumps to broken bones and concussions, and he had done so with a kind, but firm, hand.

"Well, I'm sure it's just his way," Grace said, taking up her medical bag.

"His son, on the other hand... a delightful boy. When does he return from medical school?" Miss Lawson asked.

Thomas was now training to be a doctor and had gone to London to study at the same medical school as his father had done before him. Grace was pleased for Thomas, even as she missed his companionship.

He had boarded at school in Norwich before going to London and had often returned for holidays and days off. She and Thomas had grown close, and Grace had received a letter from him that very morning, telling her of his hopes she and Doctor Mullen would come to visit him soon.

"Oh, not for a few months yet, but he'll be back," Grace replied, and Miss Lawson smiled.

"I do hope so. I'm sure he'll make a wonderful doctor," she said, bidding Grace goodbye.

As she left Miss Lawson's cottage, Grace smiled to herself. On every visit, a mention of Thomas could be guaranteed. Like Grace, he, too, had accompanied Doctor Mullen on his rounds, and had become a familiar face in the village. He was well liked, apart from by those who had a reason to dislike him.

"I do hope we go and visit him," Grace thought to herself, imagining the medical school from Thomas's descriptions, and picturing herself attending lectures and learning more about medicine.

Whilst there was little by way of practicality she had not mastered, Grace knew she lacked much of the learning necessary to be a doctor. Women could not become doctors, but it was Grace's ambition to learn as much as she could, and to this end, she had asked Doctor Mullen if she could study from his own textbooks, working in the evenings after her chores were complete. In this way, she had learned a great deal, even as she had not yet been tested in her proficiencies.

"Ah, Grace, you're back. How was Miss Lawson?" Doctor Mullen asked, as Grace entered the cottage a short while later.

"She'll be fine. I bandaged the leg and told her not to put any pressure on it. Whether she follows my advice or not, I don't know," Grace said, and Doctor Mullen laughed.

"It's the great curse of the physician—we know how to treat many illnesses, but whether the patients want to be treated is another matter," he said, and Grace smiled.

She remembered Doctor Berkley saying something similar.

"Miss Lawson was asking about Thomas. I had a letter from him this morning. He's doing well, it seems, and he's eager for us to visit him," Grace said.

Doctor Mullen smiled.

"A visit to London from the provinces? I'm not sure I'm ready to return to the metropolis after all these years of rural isolation. Though it would be nice to see him. It's been so quiet without him. I know he was often away at boarding school, but... well, I miss his company, though I have you, of course, Grace," Doctor Mullen said, and Grace smiled.

She, too, missed Thomas. They had shared so much together, and in his absence, Grace had realised how close they had become. She was proud of him, and glad to know he was following his dreams, even as she herself felt a sense of disappointment in not having the opportunity to pursue her own.

Nursing was not the respected profession of the physician, and a nurse was certainly not expected to give any form of medical opinion. A nurse could care for a patient, but it was a doctor who cured them.

"I miss him, too. I do think we should try to visit him–if you're willing, of course," Grace said, and Doctor Mullen nodded.

"I'm certainly willing, though we must hope no one in Carshalton falls ill before we can make arrangements to leave. One never knows when a doctor's services are required," Doctor Mullen replied.

Grace nodded, sitting down at the parlour table, and taking up one of her medical books. It was on anatomy, and she had been learning about the internal organs, marvelling at the pictures of the various bodily systems.

There were many who would say such pictures were not for the likes of a young woman to view, but Grace was fascinated, and she was grateful to Doctor Mullen for believing her capable of such learning.

"Isn't the human body remarkable? There's so much about it we don't understand, yet it works in such harmony. Every part has its place and role to play. It's... like it was designed," Grace said, and Doctor Mullen looked up at her and smiled.

"It was, wasn't it?" he said, raising his eyebrows.

Grace blushed. Doctor Mullen was teasing her. He was something of a freethinker and never attended church on Sundays–much to the curate's dismay.

"It's your eternal soul at risk, Doctor Mullen," the clergyman had once told him, and Doctor Mullen had retorted with a reminder of the clergyman's apparent role in the wrecking of ships off the coast.

The lights still flashed on the headland during storms, but it had been several years since any ship had followed them to its peril. Grace and Doctor Mullen kept vigil on stormy nights, and whenever a light was seen to flash, they placed another in the attic window–a sign to the would-be wreckers of their vigilance.

In this way, Grace and Doctor Mullen believed they had saved many ships from a terrible fate and halted the wrecking of ships along that lonely stretch of the Norfolk coast. But in doing so, Grace believed she was not only preventing wickedness, but atoning for the actions of her mother, too.

Mrs. Parks' words had stayed with her ever since that fateful day in the study at Carshalton House. She had come to believe they were true, for she had found no evidence to the contrary. Grace knew nothing of her real mother and father, and she feared they had perished in the wreck of *The Honoria*, the ship her adoptive mother had wrecked.

The wrecking of that ship had put a stop to Mary Carruthers' wicked ways, and those of Lady Edith, too. But try as she might, Grace could not forget the awful possibility of what her adoptive mother had done.

"*She's a murderer,*" Grace had told herself, as she had stood in front of the gravestone erected in Mary's memory.

Grace had found it hard to visit her mother–her adoptive mother–in the churchyard, and unsure of how to best remember her. Doctor Mullen had advised her to remember her for what she was–a kind and loving mother to Grace. That had been Grace's experience of her. Still, Grace's memory was tainted, as were those memories of Lady Edith, too.

"I just don't know them anymore," she had told herself, and her visits to the graves had grown less frequent, though she had continued to lay flowers on the grave of Doctor Berkley.

Doctor Mullen had been sympathetic, and he had offered to do what he could to find evidence of *The Honoria,* but to no avail. Whether Mrs. Parks was telling the truth or not, she had succeeded in poisoning Grace's memory against her mother and destroying those last precious things Grace had clung to in her times of despair.

Of her true past, Grace knew nothing, and whilst she had every assurance of a bright future ahead, the truth of who she was remained elusive.

"I JUST CAN'T FIND any details about *The Honoria.* It's as though she her name remains, and the truth lies at the bottom of the ocean," Doctor Mullen said, looking up from the pile of papers on his desk.

It was several weeks after Grace had received Thomas's letter, and Doctor Mullen had found a new lead in his search for details of Grace's past, and a number of boxes had been delivered to the cottage from a naval archive in London. Grace looked up from her medical textbook and smiled.

"Rather like me. A name without a past. If only I could remember. Why is it we don't remember memories from our early childhood? I can remember vividly those things I did when I was eight or nine, but I can't really remember anything much earlier than from about the age of five," Grace said, shaking her head with a sigh.

Doctor Mullen drew his finger and thumb over his chin, a habit he had when he was thinking.

"It's an excellent question, Grace. We know so little about early childhood development. It's such a difficult area to study, at least with any kind of large group sample. One can observe one's own children, of course. In Thomas's case, I believe he was aware at an early age, but as for remembering what he was aware of... well, that's a different matter," Doctor Mullen replied.

Grace was fascinated by memories, and she had read all of Doctor Mullen's textbooks on the subject of the mind. How a person remembers, and why a person remembers, remained a mystery. There was no given reason for the prominence of certain memories and the forgetting of others.

Try as she might, Grace could remember nothing of a shipwreck or of being found by her adoptive mother. Her first memory was as it had always been, sitting in front of the hearth in Lady's Edith's bedroom. She had felt safe there and loved. But that memory, too, was tainted, and it was one Grace tried not to dwell on.

"But do we remember everything? Is it all there waiting to be recalled?" Grace asked.

Doctor Mullen pondered for a moment.

"I suppose an imprint of everything we experience remains. It was the philosopher, John Locke, who spoke of a *"Tabula Rasa"* at birth, a blank slate on which experience is immediately chalked until the end of life. I'm not sure I entirely believe what he says–we can be certain a child is experiencing something at a certain stage during the pregnancy, but still... the mind remains a mystery, Grace, one I wish, for your sake, we could unlock," Doctor Mullen replied.

Doctor Mullen never sought to treat Grace as though she could not understand the technicalities of medicine or physiology. He explained things to her in just the same way he explained them to Thomas and was always willing to admit the limitations of his knowledge, or that of medicine itself.

There was still so much to discover, and the mind was perhaps the greatest medical mystery of them all.

"I try to remember, but I can't. I don't think it's possible. I'm told I experienced a certain set of events – the passage on the ship, the shipwreck, and my being found amidst the wreckage. But as for recalling those events... I just don't know," Grace said, closing her textbook with a sigh.

Doctor Mullen looked at her sympathetically.

"I can't promise you'll ever remember anything, Grace. But I can assure you I'm still doing what I can to find out something about where you came from. The sinking of *The Honoria* was quite an event. It wasn't just a cargo ship, but it had passengers, too–you were amongst them, and it seems you were the only survivor, though no official survivors are recorded. Your adopted mother kept you hidden, for good or ill, and the cargo was recorded as lost at sea, though we know where it really went. It was a disaster, and you're its only remnant," Doctor Mullen said, sighing, as Grace shook her head.

"I just want to know the truth, though I'm not sure if I do, either. I know that makes no sense," she said, but Doctor Mullen smiled.

"It makes perfect sense, Grace, but for now, we must return to our work. I'll continue looking through these boxes in the coming days. It's everything the archivist could find on *The Honoria*, but most of it says the same thing. I can tell you how many crates of coffee were on board, but as for the passengers, it seems they were a less valuable cargo," the doctor said, and he sighed, placing the piles of paper back into their boxes.

Grace closed her textbooks. She was grateful to Doctor Mullen, but they had been here before, following leads without ends, and always arriving back at the same point. *The Honoria* was a mystery, and from its watery grave, the answers to Grace's questions were not forthcoming.

Six years later, she was no closer to discovering the truth about her mother and father, or about where she came from. Often, she would imagine the kind of life she had been meant to have, picturing her mother and father, and dreaming of all manner of possible scenarios. Her father might have been an aristocrat, or a member of parliament, or a wealthy businessman.

Her life could have been so different, and she could only imagine what her prospects might now be had the ship not been wrecked by the very woman who had called herself her mother.

THE SURPRISING SCHOLAR

"The eleven twenty, I believe, or is it the twelve twenty? Oh, dear... no, we don't want to go to Birmingham, as remarkable a place as it is. Ah, here we are, the eleven twenty—we're in second class," Doctor Mullen said, pointing along the platform at Norwich station, to where a steaming locomotive was preparing to depart.

Grace and Doctor Mullen were on their way to London, having left Carshalton that morning, first by horse and trap, and then by carriage to Norwich station. It was a hustling, bustling place, quite different from the peaceful ravine and shoreline Grace was used to.

She was excited at the prospect of seeing London, and even more so at the prospect of seeing Thomas again. He had written several times in the past month, telling her a great deal about his lectures, and promising to show her the medical school.

"I think you'll enjoy the anatomical demonstrations. They're open to the public," he had written to tell her, and Grace was excited at the prospect of seeing something of the things she had read about in her textbooks.

"Here we are, compartment five, coach D," Grace said, opening the door for Doctor Mullen, who was struggling with the cases.

A porter came to assist them, and they were soon ensconced in the second class carriage, along with an elderly gentleman reading a newspaper, and two women who introduced themselves as the "Misses Jennings"–sisters from Ipswich.

"I always think it's so exciting travelling up to London, or should it be down to London? I'm never sure," one of them said, and Grace smiled.

She had never travelled up or down to London, and Norwich she had ever been since her arrival in Carshalton all those years ago. But the thought of London fascinated her, for she knew it was London whence *The Honoria* had set sail. Her origins lay there, and she fancied she might discover something, some clue about her past, even as she knew Doctor Mullen had done all he could to help her.

"I haven't told you this, Grace, but train travel makes me feel rather ill. I'd prefer not to talk much as we travel. I'm going to try to sleep," Doctor Mullen said, though Grace wondered if it was not also a ploy to prevent him having to talk to the twin sisters, who were now addressing the man with the newspaper about the state of the Empire in the far east.

"Why do they persist in empire building? I simply don't understand it, and as for Canada..." one of them was saying.

Grace smiled to herself, taking out one of her textbooks and opening it, hoping to pass the journey, studying the anatomy of the body, rather than the anatomy of empire. She had never been on a train before, and it astonished her to think of the engine pulling along with it a dozen carriages, as now it huffed and puffed its way out of the station.

The two Miss Jennings soon realised the man behind the newspaper was more interested in reading the news than discussing it, and they took out their embroidery, whilst Doctor Mullen kept his eyes resolutely closed.

Grace found the motion of the train somewhat startling, and she was unable to read, the words on the page moving up and down in a strange and nausea inducing manner.

"Oh, dear, perhaps I'm like Doctor Mullen," she thought to herself, closing the textbook, and looking out of the window.

They were passing across the flat Norfolk fens, the great vista of the sky stretching out towards the sea. It was fascinating to watch, and despite her queasiness, Grace could not take her eyes off the ever-changing view.

The fenland gave way to farmland, and they stopped at several small stations, where passengers got on and off, before continuing their journey towards London. It was several hours before they reached the outskirts of the capital, and Grace was astonished at the extent of the urban sprawl, with its closely packed houses and smoke belching chimneys.

She knew little of London, and she could hardly believe the way in which people lived there–cheek by jowl.

"Disease must be rife," she thought to herself, remembering some of the studies she had read about clean drinking water and the dangers of communal pumps, pumping dirty sewage from the river.

"We'll be arriving at Saint Pancras shortly," the conductor said, opening the door of the compartment.

Doctor Mullen opened his eyes immediately.

"Oh, goodness me, are we there already? I've slept the whole journey long," he exclaimed, and Grace smiled as the two sisters exchanged glances.

The man with the newspaper had not uttered a single word since being left to his own devices, and now he folded his periodical and nodded to them.

"Good day to you," he said, stepping out of the compartment as the train came to a halt.

"Come along, Grace, the porter can fetch our bags. Good day to you, ladies," Doctor Mullen said, ushering Grace out of the compartment.

"That was quite remarkable. I've never travelled by train," she said, and Doctor Mullen smiled.

"Ah, yes—I hadn't thought of that. Well, here we are, in London. Let's get to our lodgings. I'm sure you're feeling quite tired after your journey," he said.

But Grace was wide awake, and eager to see the sights of London. They took a carriage from the station, and Doctor Mullen instructed the driver to take a roundabout route to their lodgings, which were close to the medical school in Bloomsbury.

They saw Buckingham Palace, and the Houses of Parliament, along with parks and gardens, grand central streets and boule-vards, and buildings such as Grace had never imagined. London was built on a vast scale, a heaving metropolis, and she feared she would never find any of the answers she was seeking there.

"It's an extraordinary place," she said, as the carriage pulled up in front of the lodgings Doctor Mullen had engaged for them during their time in the capital.

A handsome townhouse was divided into apartments, and theirs was on the second floor. Grace climbed down, helping Doctor Mullen, just as an excited cry came from across the street.

"Father, Grace. You're here! How marvellous!" Thomas exclaimed, and he hurried across, dodging an oncoming hansom cab, as Grace ran to greet him.

"It's been quite a journey," she exclaimed, as she slung her arms around him and kissed him.

"I'm so glad to see you both. I've just finished my lectures for the day. We've been dissecting hearts, pig's hearts, but still," he said, as Doctor Mullen came to greet him.

"A messy business, and you're still splattered," he said,

glancing down at Thomas's waistcoat, where the marks of the dissection were plain to see.

Thomas blushed.

"I haven't had a chance to change. I knew you'd be arriving at any moment. Let me help you get your things inside. What news from Carshalton? Are the patients their usual selves?" he asked, as he picked up two of their cases and led them up a flight of steps to the door of the house.

It was opened by a maid, and they were directed to the second floor and given keys to the apartment.

"The patients are behaving themselves with the usual unruliness. They ask where Thomas is. Don't they, Grace?" Doctor Mullen said, and Grace smiled.

"That's right, they do. You're certainly missed for your bedside manner," she said, and Thomas laughed.

"It doesn't make much difference here. We cut things up, we learn how they're put together, and we try to put them back in some semblance of order. As for patients... well, I haven't seen one since I arrived. None of my fellow students knows anything about real patients. They're always amazed when I speak from experience. I've seen so many illnesses in Carshalton. It really is a study in itself," Thomas replied.

They had entered the apartment now, a well-furnished sitting room, replete with large pot plants, and ornate peacock wallpaper presented itself, with two doors on either side, leading to bedrooms and a small kitchen. Their meals would be prepared for them and brought by the maid, and it seemed they would be very comfortable for the duration of their stay.

"And a fine view from the window, too," Doctor Mullen said, pulling back the lace nets and peering out across the square.

"Are your lodgings close?" Grace asked, and Thomas nodded.

"Yes, just across from here, not far at all. I'll show you them. I want to show you everything," he said, even as Doctor Mullen sat down wearily by the hearth, where a fire had been kindled to warm the room.

"I'm quite exhausted by the journey. I think I'll send for some tea and toast and catch a sleep before dinner," he said.

"But you'll come with me, won't you, Grace?" Thomas asked, and Grace nodded.

She had not come all the way to London to doze in a chair by the fire. Everything was new and exciting, and she readily agreed to accompany Thomas on a walk around the university and medical school.

The day was warm, and the late afternoon sun shone brightly as they walked across the square, past handsome buildings, ornate statues, and scholars hurrying back and forth between their lodgings and the library.

"It's magnificent," Grace said, even as she knew it was a world she could never make her own.

There were no women at the university, only men, and the medical school was the same. Women could not attain a degree, however hard they studied and worked. It was a painful truth, even as Grace had no intention of ceasing her studies.

She learned because she wanted to, and despite her adoptive mother's failing, Grace still held the same ambition she had always done. She wanted to be a nurse, and to help others as she believed a nurse should do.

"This is the medical library," Thomas said, pointing to an impressive building built in white marble, with colonnades and large windows, through which Grace could see towering bookshelves rising to the ceiling.

"If only I could spend a few hours in there. I've got so many questions, but I've exhausted your father's textbooks. I want to know more about memories and how they're unlocked," Grace said.

She had told Thomas some of this in her letters, and now he listened with interest as she explained some of her theories about the mind as they sat on the steps of the library.

"I see, so you're surmising we all retain our memories, but it's unlocking them that matters," he said, as Grace's explanation came to an end.

"Precisely. Think about a time when a particular scent or taste gives rise to a memory previously hidden. I'm certain any memory can be triggered with the right stimulus. But whether I can ever remember my own memories... well, I don't know," Grace said, shaking her head sadly.

Thomas put his arm around her.

"You're quite remarkable, Grace. You know more about the mind — about anything to do with medicine — than any of the scholars here," Thomas said, pointing to the groups of students scurrying back and forth.

Grace blushed. He was always quick to praise her, even as she felt her own knowledge to be entirely lacking compared to his and Doctor Mullen's.

"I just... read the textbooks, but it's watching your father at work that really teaches me. It was the same with Doctor Berkley. I don't think you can learn much about medicine from a textbook, though I'm sure there're plenty here who'd disagree," Grace said, but Thomas shook his head.

"No, you're right. You're absolutely right. You can learn something of the theoretical side from a textbook, but the practicalities... no. Until you've set a broken leg, or seen a patient with measles, you can't say you've actually experienced something of what it's like," he replied.

They walked on now, discussing life in Carshalton and Thomas's new life in London. He was keen to hear more about Grace's search for the truth concerning her mother and father, and the talk inevitably turned to the wreckers.

"There hasn't been a wreck for some years, and certainly not in the months since you've been here. They know we're watching them, and whenever we see a light shone from the headland, we place our own lamp in the attic window. Theirs soon goes out, but... I worry now we're away. What if a storm blow up and ship sails along the Devil's Way? What then?" she asked, shuddering at the thought of the wreckers making preparation for their wickedness.

"It's got to stop, eventually. But it's proving it that's the hard thing. Ships are wrecked off that coast, with or without a light to confuse their captains. And Captain Dickinson was right. Carshalton headland is the perfect place for gathering moths at night," Thomas said, sighing, as they now came to the steps of Doctor Mullen's and Grace's lodgings.

"Will I see you in the morning?" Thomas asked, and Grace nodded.

"Certainly, I'd like to accompany you to one of the lectures, if I may," she said, and Thomas grinned.

"It's an operation tomorrow. They're amputating a leg," he said, and Grace nodded.

"Excellent, I'll be glad to see it," she said, and Thomas laughed.

"There aren't many women who'd say that," he said, and Grace shrugged.

"I suppose I'm not really like other women," she replied.

"And I wouldn't change it for the world," he said, slipping his hand into hers and squeezing it.

Grace blushed. She had missed him terribly, and she was only too glad to have his company again.

"I'll see you tomorrow," she said, smiling at him, before hurrying up the steps and turning to wave to him as she rang the bell.

He stayed standing at the bottom of the steps, and as the maid opened the door, he called out a final farewell.

"I forgot to tell you–you look very pretty in that dress," he said, causing her to blush even further.

* * *

THE NEXT MORNING, Doctor Mullen was still feeling tired, and he told Grace he would remain at their lodgings to rest.

"You're not unwell, are you, Doctor Mullen?" Grace asked, for she was concerned he looked somewhat pale after their journey.

But the doctor dismissed her concerns, insisting she meet Thomas as planned. Grace decided not to eat breakfast, knowing the subject of the operation to come. She was curious to see it and had read up on the procedure the night before.

Thomas had told her the operation was to be an amputation, a limb requiring removal due to infection. Grace had never witnessed such a procedure before, for the rudiments of country medicine were nothing compared to that treated in hospitals such as this. She was fascinated at the prospect, if a little nervous.

"Tell me all about it when you get back. It's a long time since I witnessed anything like that," Doctor Mullen said, bidding Grace goodbye.

She met Thomas near the library steps. He was smartly dressed in a frock coat and tails, and smiled at her as she approached.

"I hope your stomach's ready for this," he said, and Grace smiled.

"Is yours?" she replied.

Despite not having seen such a bloody operation, Grace had seen her share of unpleasantness over the years. Country medicine was not entirely dull and as they entered the lecture theatre, she looked around her with interest. An operating table was set up in the centre, whilst on three sides, raised seating allowed the spectators to view the proceedings.

Another table was set with various implements, and the floor was stained with blood marks, the sign of past procedures. Grace and Thomas took seats one row back, whilst others, too, filed in. There were no other women present, and several of the other students whispered critically.

"You shouldn't bring a lady here, Thomas. She'll faint," one of them said, leaning forward to chastise Thomas, who smiled.

"Oh, I think you'll find she's got a stronger stomach than you, Ernest. There's not a lot my friend Grace doesn't know about medicine," Thomas said, glancing at Grace, who smiled.

She felt excited to be there, excited at the prospect of seeing a real operation for herself. Now, the surgeon entered, introducing himself as Doctor McKirahan, a senior surgeon, with a white beard and keen, bright eyes, who would be performing the amputation of the leg, and talking through the procedure as he did so.

The patient was now brought in, dressed in a white gown, and lifted from a wheelchair onto the operating table. He looked terrified, but it was clear as to the purpose of the operation. His leg was red and swollen, and a fever was gripping him.

"Sometimes, an operation like this becomes necessary. It's always the last resort. But if a fever can't be stemmed, it must be stopped. The fever travels up the leg. We've caught it before it passes the knee, thus, by removing the lower leg, we'll prevent it spreading further," Doctor McKirahan said.

A murmur of agreement went up around the room, which was now full of interested spectators.

"Are they are all medical students?" Grace asked, but Thomas shook his head.

"No, not all. Some people just enjoy the spectacle," he replied, as the patient was now strapped to the bed and given a block of wood to bite down on.

"We use chloroform to anaesthetise the patient. But too much can be lethal, too little can result in excessive pain," Doctor McKirahan said, as now the noxious substance was applied to the patient with a cloth, causing his body to go limp.

"Extraordinary," Thomas said, shaking his head.

The doctor was now taking up the necessary tools, assisted by several helpers, and the spectators were leaning forward, whispering to one another in awed anticipation of what was to come.

"The procedure has to be swift, and every cut necessary and anticipated," the doctor continued.

Grace watched the patient's face, his eyes closed, the block of wood clamped tightly between his jaws. His head was lolled to one side, the chloroform-soaked cloth held close by one of the assistants, ready to apply as soon as the first cut was made. Grace gripped the wooden rail in front of her, hardly daring to watch, and yet unable to avert her gaze.

"I don't think I could do it," Thomas whispered, as now Doctor McKirahan made the first incision.

The patient reacted instinctively, his limbs tensing, his hands flailing. He let out a cry, as the assistant held the chloroform to his face.

"And again, continue, swiftly and methodically," the doctor said.

Gasps of revulsion went up around the theatre, even as necks were craned to see the extraordinary spectacle taking place.

"A woman shouldn't be seeing this," the student who had early chastised Thomas exclaimed.

Grace turned to him. He looked pale, as though he was about to be sick.

"It seems I've got a far stronger stomach than you. Perhaps you should be the one to step outside," she retorted, and several of the other laughed.

"She's got you there, Ernest," another said, and Ernest was promptly sick.

Grace turned back to the operating table, where the surgeon had just completed his grim task. The speed at which he worked was extraordinary, and now the limb was severed, and another assistant was packing the wound with bandages. Doctor McKirahan stood back triumphantly as a round of applause went up from the gathered crowd.

"Remarkable," Thomas said, shaking his head.

"A successful amputation–swift, and with the least possible pain to the patient. We continue to apply the chloroform whilst the bleeding is stemmed. The wound begins to heal slowly, but what of infection? How do prevent the possibility?" Doctor McKirahan asked.

"Cleanliness," one student called out, and the doctor nodded.

"Yes, bathing the wound and keeping it clean. And what else?" he asked.

There was silence now, and the doctor looked around him in exasperation. But Grace knew the answer. At least, she thought she did, and she raised her hand, even as Thomas looked at her in surprise.

"I believe Doctor Joseph Lister is making considerable progress in the practice of antiseptics," she said.

Doctor McKirahan looked at Grace and smiled.

"That's exactly right. Can you tell us more about antiseptics?" he asked, and Grace rose nervously to her feet.

"It's only what I've read, and perhaps I've not understood it fully, but Doctor Lister has discovered that carbolic acid kills the dirt in a wound. He applies a spray of the substance to procedures, thus lessening the threat of infection," Grace replied.

The doctor nodded.

"That's precisely correct. I have carbolic acid here, the bandages are soaked in it. It'll help keep the wound clean, along with water, too. Yes, very good. I'm surprised... it's rare for a woman to enter my lecture room. But it seems you weren't perturbed by the sights you saw, and you've put my students to shame with your knowledge of Doctor Lister's new methods," he said.

Grace blushed. She had read about carbolic acid in a medical journal belonging to Thomas's father. It was all very new, but Doctor Mullen had used carbolic acid to clean a wound inflicted by a horse on a groom back in Carshalton, and Grace had seen the effects for herself.

"It's just something I've read about," Grace replied, and the doctor nodded.

"Very impressive. Anyway, we'll reconvene in a week. I'll be removing an ingrowing toenail from a patient just returned from the New World. It'll be an interesting procedure. In the meantime, continue studying your anatomical textbooks, noting the parts of the body suitable for amputation and the manner in which infections can spread. You're dismissed," Doctor McKirahan said, returning his attentions to the patient, who was now recovering from the effects of the chloroform.

The other student and spectators filed out, and Thomas turned to Grace and smiled.

"You certainly impressed him," he said, and Grace blushed.

"I only repeated what I'd read and what I'd seen your father do," she said, and Thomas smiled.

"Well, that's the foundation of medical study, learning and watching," he said, as they made their way out of the lecture room, but Grace sighed and shook her head.

"But it doesn't mean I'll ever be a doctor, does it?" she replied.

Grace had been caught up in the excitement of the operation, imagining herself as the surgeon or one of the doctors. But despite all she knew about medicine, far more than many of those gathered to watch the operation that day, she would never be the doctor she longed to be. A nurse could only do so much, and whilst Grace was glad to be fulfilling that which she had always dreamed of, she could not help but want something more...

HALLOWED HALLS

*A*s they emerged from the lecture room, Doctor McKirahan was supervising the removal of the newly amputated patient.

"You'll be perfectly all right. The wound will soon heal, and then we can begin teaching you to walk on the crutches," he was saying as the man was wheeled away by one of the assistants, still with his head lolled to one side, the result of the continued effects of the chloroform.

As the doctor turned, he caught sight of Grace and Thomas, beckoning to them with a smile on his face.

"It was a remarkable operation, Doctor McKirahan," Thomas said, and the doctor shrugged.

"A standard enough procedure, but a less than standard response to my question from this young lady? Tell me, how do you know of such things, miss...?" he asked, and Grace blushed.

"Grace Carruthers, Doctor McKirahan. I... well, I've been helping Doctor Mullen–Thomas's father–for many years. And before that, I helped our previous village doctor, Doctor Tobias Berkley. My mother was a nurse, you see, and... well, I wanted to be a nurse, too. I can't be a doctor, I know that. But I've learned as much as I could," she said, feeling suddenly very foolish.

Women did not become doctors. It was impossible. For all her learning, all her experience, all her determination, Grace would be forever an assistant. Her sex precluded her from anything else.

"I was impressed. And you say it's Thomas's father who's taught you these things? Doctor Mullen and I go back a long way. You're an interesting young woman, Grace. It's unfortunate I can't admit you to the medical school. I'd certainly like to. It's not every day one finds a woman who can stomach an amputation then answer a question no one else knows the answer to. Even my best student, young Thomas, here," the doctor said, glancing at Thomas who laughed.

"I've learned a great deal from Grace over the years, too. She knows more than anyone about medicine," he replied.

Grace was flattered, but it did not change the facts. She would never be a doctor, despite her longing to be so. They exchanged further pleasantries with Doctor McKirahan before the surgeon was called away, and Grace and Thomas were left standing in the grand entrance hallway of the medical school. It was an imposing place, decorated with murals depicting the history of medicine through the ages, stretching back to the ancient Greeks and Romans, to Hippocrates and Galen.

"Would you like me to show you around? It's a fascinating building. We could see the library and the lecture rooms, and I can show you the anatomy gallery," Thomas said.

Grace was interested to see whatever he was able to show her. She liked spending time with Thomas, and she missed him dreadfully now he was away at medical school.

"I'd be delighted," she said, and he led her through the corridors, pointing out the various departments and expertise of those inhabiting them.

"That's where they study tropical diseases. It's quite remarkable what gets brought back from far-flung parts of the world. And this is the anatomy gallery," he said, opening a door leading onto a wide corridor, where several dozen skeletons were displayed.

Grace was fascinated, and she stood in front of the first construction, peering at the skull as Thomas explained the various parts of the skeleton to her.

"We're such delicate creatures, aren't we?" she said, and Thomas smiled.

"And we're discovering more about ourselves every day. Look at the bone construction, how every part is fixed to another. There's a perfect harmony there. It's no wonder medicine was one based entirely on the balance of the parts," he said, as they walked past the other skeletons, each with its own distinctive size and shape.

Grace was fascinated, but this was a world she could never hope to inhabit for herself, a world she knew she would soon have to leave. Thomas would make a fine doctor, just like his father, but Grace did not know where her own destiny lay, and her life to come would be like.

She could not remain forever as Doctor Mullen's assistant, and yet she had discovered a natural gift for healing and helping others.

"I just wish... I knew who I was," Grace said, as they left the anatomy gallery behind and continued their tour of the medical school.

"It can't be easy, I know. But... you know who you are. You know who you are now, I mean. You're Grace Carruthers, nurse and medial expert, assistant to Doctor Christopher Mullen, of Carshalton, Norfolk," he said, and Grace smiled.

"Aren't you forgetting something? Dearest Friend to Mr. Thomas Mullen, the great medical student, set to make discoveries beyond the wildest dreams of science and greater than those of anything discovered before," Grace said, and Thomas laughed.

"But I've just had the most wonderful idea," he said, and Grace looked at him in surprise.

"What do you mean?" she asked, and he smiled.

"Well… you could be my assistant. I don't mean as a nurse, I mean as a doctor. I know you can't be a real doctor, but you know more than anyone about medicine, including me. We could work together. Think of the things we might discover–a way to use chloroform safely for absolute pain relief, a method of applying antiseptic during operations, the ability to… I don't know, take the organs from one person, and put them into another. I know it's the work of dreams, but… can you imagine what we could do?" he said.

Grace smiled. His enthusiasm was infectious, but behind his invitation, it seemed there was more than just the hope of a professional relationship. She reached out and took his hand in hers, and he blushed, perhaps realising the extent of his enthusiasm.

"I think it's a wonderful idea," she replied, and he smiled back at her.

"I… well, perhaps you know how I feel about you, Grace. We grew up together, but… that doesn't mean I don't have… feelings for you. I love you," he admitted, and Grace rested her forehead against his.

"I love you, too," she said, surprised at the ease with which each of them was able to utter those words.

Grace did not know when she had first realized her feelings for him. They had grown gradually and comfortably. But there was no doubt in her mind as to her feelings for him. She loved him, and now, it seemed, he had realised the same feelings for her.

"How glad I am to hear you say so. I thought… well, I didn't know. We've lived a strange life, you and I. You, especially. I wasn't sure if... well, I don't know what your plans for the future might be," he said, and Grace smiled.

"I didn't have any plans, and we should keep the matter to ourselves for now. I'm not sure what your father would say," Grace replied, for she felt Doctor Mullen may not approve of a courting couple under his roof, albeit only in the holidays.

Thomas nodded.

"I've still got to pass my examinations and finish medical school. But I meant what I said, Grace. We could work together. It would be the ideal partnership, don't you think? You can continue studying in Carshalton, and I'll be here in London. We'll see one another as often as we can, and when the time comes... we'll tell him," he said, and Grace smiled.

She could not help but feel a sense of happiness at these words, even as she had imagined Thomas marrying the daughter of a wealthy surgeon, or even being too wedded to his work to consider matters of matrimony. She wondered how long he had been considering the idea of such a proposal, or whether it had come on him suddenly and in haste. He slipped his hand into hers and squeezed it.

"Come now, I've still got so much to show you, and then we could go to an excellent coffee house I know. It's not far from here, and they serve the most delicious cakes," he said, leading her along the corridor past a statue of Hippocrates.

Returning to the entrance hall, they found a class just finishing, and a chatter of excited medical student discussing the topic loudly.

"I don't see why we should treat ailments of the mind any different to that of the body. It's an illness to be cured like any others," one was saying, but another scorned him.

"Then are you saying a criminal should be treated rather than punished? Think of the madman who kills his entire family. Are we to final sympathy for a murderer and offer him a tonic and a warm hospital bed, rather than the hangman's noose?" he exclaimed.

It fascinated Grace to hear such conversations, even as she knew there were those who would say such things were not for a woman's ears.

"Look at this, Grace, the names of the famous doctors trained at the school. I'm sure my father will find his name here one day, after he's died, of course," Thomas said, pointing to a large wooden board, on which were engraved dozens of names in gold relief.

Grace looked through them with interest. There were names she recognized from the books and journals she read, Costin, Bamburgh, Allinson... all with their dates and place of birth and death. Some came with an epitaph–"*Hero of the Brixton cholera epidemic*" or "*Killed in action in France.*"

It was an homage to the many men who served faithfully in their vocation as doctors and surgeons. But as she looked down the names, one in particular caught her eye–"*Professor Sir Anstruther Thornberry, surgeon, lost at sea, Norfolk, 1858,*" she read, pointing to it, and looking in surprise at Thomas, who leaned down to examine the entry more closely.

"Isn't it strange?" Grace said, even as she had no reason for believing a connection to herself.

But there *was* something interesting in the words. Professor Thornberry had been lost at sea–shipwrecked, and the ship had been lost off the Norfolk coast. But it was the year Grace was drawn to 1858, the year of her birth...

"How very curious. I wonder... well, you don't think it might be the same ship you were being carried on, do you?" Thomas asked, and Grace shook her head.

"I don't know. But it could be, couldn't it?" she said, feeling a sudden urge to investigate further and discover more about Professor Thornberry and the lost ship.

"There's an archive here–a fairly comprehensive one. They

keep details of every former student at the medical school. They're bound to have an account of the shipwreck there, and perhaps details of the passengers, too," Thomas said, a note of excitement entering his voice.

Grace could not take her eyes away from the inscription on the board, and the more she looked at it, reading the words over and over again, the more convinced she was as to a possible connection. She had never heard the name of Thornberry before, but there was something about it, something familiar.

"Can we look there? Can we find the details about him? He might've known my parents. If it names the ship, perhaps..." Grace said, as any number of possibilities occurred to her.

She had long given up any hope of discovering the truth about herself or her origins. All she had known was deceit and lies. Her mother... Lady Edith... the wreckers...

"If it's there to be found, we'll find it," Thomas said, beckoning Grace to follow him, and as they hurried towards the library, Grace could not help but feel as though a new chapter in her life was beginning. Her feelings for Thomas growing ever stronger, and the possibility of the truth lying before her.

THE ARCHIVES

"Can I help you?" the man sitting behind the desk asked, peering at them over a pair of half-moon spectacles.

Grace and Thomas glanced at one another.

"I want to look in the archives," Thomas replied, and the man's eyes narrowed.

"In the archives? And do you have permission to do so?" he asked.

"I'm a medical student here. I used the library every day. I've got my credentials here," Thomas replied, pulling out a crumpled piece of paper with several signatures on it.

The man looked down at it and shook his head.

"Only researchers can use the archives," he replied, with the arrogance of a man who knows his position and the rules governing it.

"But I need access to the archives," Thomas replied, even as the man shook his head.

"Not without the written permission of a senior member of the faculty, I won't..." he began, but footsteps now approached, the archivist looking up in surprise, and Grace turned to find Doctor McKirahan standing behind them.

"Is there a problem?" he asked, and the archivist cleared his throat.

"No problem, sir, no. I was just explaining to this... student the rules concerning the archives," he said.

Doctor McKirahan smiled.

"Ah, yes, I'm glad to see them both here. They're conducting some important research on my behalf. I hope you'll afford them every assistance," he said, smiling at Grace, who could happily have thrown her arms around him and embraced him.

The archivist appeared taken aback.

"But, sir..." he stammered.

"Carry on, Palin, let them in. It's imperative I have my information as soon as possible. Lives depend on it. Isn't that what we do here? We make discoveries, and you're at the forefront of that, Palin. Don't let me down," he called out, ambling away with a smile on his face.

The archivist knew he was defeated, and grudgingly, he showed Grace and Thomas into the archives, where rows of shelves stretched in every direction, covered in dusty books and box files.

"What do you want to look at?" the archivist asked.

"We're looking for information on a Professor Sir Anstruther Thornberry. He was a graduate of the medical school, listed on the roll of honour. We want information on how he died–there was a shipwreck," Thomas said, and the archivist nodded.

He went off muttering to himself, returning a short while later with several files and a bound volume resting on top. They were dusty, and as he handed them over, Grace sneezed.

"These can't have been opened in years," she exclaimed.

"You can examine them over there. But I'll be watching you," the archivist said.

Thomas gave him a withering look, and he and Grace made

their way over to a table by the window, laying out the files and the volume to examine. It was a set of letters, correspondence between the professor and various other medical authorities. He had led a remarkable life, travelling all over the world in pursuit of his research into tropical medicine.

"Look at the places these letters are stamped from, India, South Africa, Australia. Is there anywhere he didn't go?" Thomas said, shaking his head in astonishment.

Grace was fascinated, and now she opened the first of the box files, finding various drawings and sketches of far-off places, along with further letters to the professor's wife.

"She was called Lucy. It's clear he loved her very much. I wonder... do you think she's still alive?" Grace asked, searching through the piles of papers in search of the evidence she needed.

There was so much to look through — letters, journals, clippings from newspapers and periodicals, but it was the information on the shipwreck she wanted to discover.

How had the professor died? Had his wife been on board at the time? So many accounts had been given, and Grace knew she could not trust Mrs. Parks' account of what had happened on that fateful night.

"Look at this, here it is, *The Honoria*," Thomas said, holding up what appeared to be a newspaper clipping.

With trembling hands, Grace took the piece of paper and began to read. It was an account of the shipwreck in which the professor had drowned. *The Honoria* had been wrecked off the Norfolk coast at...

"Carshalton," Grace exclaimed as she continued to read.

A cargo ship with passengers... bound for Glasgow... all hands lost... including the eminent and respected Professor Sir Anstruther Thornberry, along with his daughter, a baby of a mere six weeks... Grace stared at Thomas in astonishment.

"You mean to say... you're the daughter of Professor Thornberry, one of the greatest doctors this school has ever produced?" Thomas exclaimed.

Grace could hardly believe it, either. And yet here was the evidence in black and white. Further searches through the boxes revealed a list of passengers on the ship, and the professor was listed as travelling with his daughter, and a nurse named Lilian.

There was no mention of Lady Thornberry, and it seemed the professor had taken his daughter with him alone, perhaps intending to meet his wife in the north at a later date.

"But look, I'm not listed as Grace. I'm named as Charlotte Thornberry," Grace said, convinced she had discovered the truth about herself and her past.

No other children were listed, and certainly no babies. The dates matched, and if it was believed, everyone on board had perished...

"There'd be no reason to search for you. Your mother... the nurse, could easily have kept you secret. No one was looking for you," Thomas said, as Grace shook her head in astonishment.

It was extraordinary, and yet here was the evidence lying before her. Her father was Professor Thornberry. He had taken her by ship to Newcastle, and the wreckers had driven them onto the rocks.

The professor had been drowned, and a miracle had seen Grace washed up on the beach, only to be discovered very person responsible for her father's death.

"I... I never thought, but... it's too extraordinary," Grace said, and Thomas put his arm around her.

"But aren't you pleased to know the truth? I know it's difficult, but wouldn't you rather know, than be forever wondering about it?" he asked.

Grace nodded. She was glad to know the truth, and to find the identity she had long since believed to be lost. But the fact of her discovery now gave rise to further questions, chief amongst them, the identity of her birth mother.

"Do you think she's still alive?" Grace asked, and Thomas shrugged his shoulders.

"I don't know, but why shouldn't she be? She'd have been a young woman at the time, a young widow, distraught to lose her husband and child. I'm sure we could find her. We could ask my father and Doctor McKirahan. They're bound to know if Lady Thornberry's still alive," Thomas said.

Amongst the items in the archive was a charcoal sketch. It showed a handsome man, with a defined jawline, wide eyes, a high nose, and with just the faintest hint of a beard. It was signed by the professor himself, and as Grace held it in her hands, she knew she was staring into the eyes of her father. It was the strangest of feelings, and she could hardly bear to tear herself away.

"I want to know everything about him," she said, and Thomas smiled.

"Then let's find your mother," he said as they packed away the archive materials, leaving only the sketch remaining.

Thomas glanced over his shoulder to where the archivist was sitting with his back to them. Swiftly, he placed the charcoal sketch in his notebook, slipping it into his pocket and smiling.

"Thomas, we can't..." Grace whispered, but the deed was done, and he took her by the hand and rose to his feet.

"We're finished here, thank you," he said, and the archivist looked up and nodded.

"You're fortunate Doctor McKirahan was passing. I trust you found everything you needed," he said, and Grace and Thomas nodded.

"Far more, in fact," Grace replied, still unable to believe her good fortune in this monumental discovery.

As they left the archives, Grace felt a burden had been

lifted from her. She knew the truth about her past, the past she had long believed to be lost. It was extraordinary to think of the life she might have lived had *The Honoria* not been wrecked off the Norfolk coast. She pictured her father, realising there was nothing else she could have been but a student of medicine.

"Are you certain about this?" Doctor Mullen asked, when Grace and Thomas had given their explanation of what they had discovered.

"As certain as we can be, it all fits together. The shipwreck, the baby, the belief all hands were lost, the account from that wicked woman, Mrs. Parks. It all makes sense," Grace said, and Thomas's father shook his head in astonishment.

"I'm amazed. I remember the professor. He was a brilliant mind. Far beyond any of the rest of us. He was the youngest professor of tropical medicine ever appointed at the university. And I remember the shipwreck now, too. But I never made the connection to Carshalton. And his wife... yes, Lady Lucy Thornberry. She was a dear creature. I'm sure she's still alive," Doctor Mullen said, and Grace glanced at Thomas, feeling both elated and fearful at the news.

To think her mother was still alive was a remarkable, yet terrifying prospect. Would she even believe Grace was who she said she was? There was little proof, if any, as to what she was saying.

Grace had no desire for material gain. She simply wanted to know the truth–about her parents, about what her life might have been like, about what the future might hold.

"Do you think... well, is there the possibility of finding her, do you think?" Grace asked, glancing at Thomas, who gave her a reassuring smile.

"I don't see why not. I can make enquiries. I'm sure she'll still be in London. But perhaps she's married again, or... well, you should prepare yourself for the possibility she mightn't be alive, but if she is... well, what a happy reunion you'll have," Doctor Mullen said.

Grace was overwhelmed at the prospect of finally meeting her mother. She had long since dismissed the possibility as idle fantasy, believing her mother to be dead or long since disappeared. But with such a tangible hope now in her heart, Grace could not help but feel elated at the possibility of what was to come. Her mother might yet be alive, and she would be able to tell her all about her father and the life they might have led had the ship not been wrecked.

"I'm sorry to ask you this, Grace. But I'm curious... how do you feel about Mary Carruthers?" Thomas asked, when later they walked together in the gardens of the medical school.

Grace glanced at him and sighed. She had been considering the question for herself, and it was one she found the answer to confusing. Had it not been for the woman she had so long considered being her mother–assumed to be, and with perfectly good reason–she would not be alive.

Had it not been for the actions of Mary Carruthers and the other wreckers, she would still be alive, as would her father, and her life would have been immeasurably different. At the moment of the shipwreck, a new course was chosen for her, a choice which she was yet still living out the consequences of.

"I don't know," she admitted, and he slipped his hand into hers and squeezed it.

"I didn't mean to upset you," he said, but she shook her head.

"I'm not upset, and you're right to ask me. It's something I've thought a great deal about, but I don't have an answer. I'd resigned myself to never finding the truth. I thought I'd grow old in a sort of limbo. I couldn't think of her as my mother, and yet I can't help but feel a connection to her. I always told others I wanted to be a nurse because of the example of my moth–of Mary. But after I learned the truth... well, she's hardly an example of someone who did good, is she?" Grace replied.

She felt torn between what she now knew of Mary and the example she had seen in her. Mary had been a nurse. She had been faultless in her care of Lady Edith, and yet Lady Edith, too, had been implicated in the wicked circumstances of Grace's father's death.

It was likely neither of them ever knew the truth about Grace's parents–nor her true name, Charlotte. As for calling herself that, Grace was undecided. It would be like putting on an entirely new identity, and there was still so much of her past she wanted to retain.

"You're not like her, not at all. Don't ever believe yourself capable of doing what she did. I know they say the sins of the fathers... but it's not like that," Thomas said, raising Grace's hand to his lips.

But Grace shook her head. She was not worried about that. She had come to terms with what her mother had done, and she knew she would never be capable of following in her footsteps. But the discovery of her parents, of her father and mother, of the tragedy they had endured, had changed something.

Another life was waiting for her, one she was yet to discover, but with it came the possibility of rejection. Grace had lost so much in her short life, and the possibility of her mother, her true mother, not wishing to see her, or even calling her a liar and a fraud was very real.

"I know it's not. I'm not worried about that. I'm just... anxious about meeting my mother. I know your father's going to do his best to find her, and I hope he does, but... what if she doesn't want to know me? What if she's already grieved for me, and left me in the past? There might be other children, too. It's a possibility, don't you think?" she said, and Thomas nodded.

"We all face the possibility of rejection, don't we? I was... worried myself," he said, gazing into Grace's eyes.

She blushed, shaking her head. He was being foolish if he thought she would reject him. Thomas had been nothing but kind and loving towards her, their feelings for one another growing stronger with every passing season.

"You didn't need to be," she said.

"And neither should you be, either. But you can only try, Grace. Don't be afraid. We'll find your mother, and if she wants to believe your story, so be it. But if she doesn't, don't you already have a family? My father and I," he said, and Grace smiled.

He was right. Doctor Mullen, like Doctor Berkley before him, had been like a father to her. And Thomas... he had been a brother, a friend, and now...

"I do, yes, and I wouldn't change anything about it. And perhaps that's why I should be grateful to Mary Carruthers for what she did. Looking back, I see the fullness of my life, and had it not been for the shipwreck, you and I would never have met, and I'd not be standing here with you at my side," she said, as he slipped his arms around her, and she rested her head on his chest.

"Things happen for a reason, Grace. I'm convinced of that. It's not always something we understand at the time. You've lived quite a life, but now's the time for answers, and I'm certain we'll find them," he replied.

Grace looked up at him and smiled. He seemed suddenly very grown up, and she could imagine him as the doctor he was now training to be. In her mind, she pictured the two of them together, making a grand medical discovery, or simply helping others with the combination of their knowledge and skill.

Grace felt proud to be in his arms, and contented, too. Thomas was right. Whether her mother accepted her or not, she had made a family for herself. Blood ties were not the only ties that mattered, far from it, and in Thomas and Doctor Mullen, Grace had found all the family she needed.

"I think we should tell your father of our plans, if we're to marry, or..." Grace said, her words trailing off, for she did not know entirely what to expect of this new and unexpected turn of events.

He smiled at her and kissed her on the forehead.

"One thing at a time. Let's find your mother first. She mightn't approve of me," he said, laughing as he put his arm around her.

Dusk was falling, and as they bid one another farewell outside Grace's and Doctor Mullen's lodgings, he stole a kiss from her, even as a lamp burning in the upper room suggested his father had not yet retired to bed.

"I'll see you in the morning," she said, and he nodded.

"I've got a lecture to go to first thing. I'm afraid it's only for the medical students. We're dissecting a pig's kidney," he said, and Grace laughed.

"You can tell me all about it over luncheon–let's just hope we're not served offal," she said, and Thomas laughed.

"We dissected lungs last week, then I was served them in a ghastly pie at an inn on Shepperton Street. No, I think we can do better than pig's kidneys. We'll dine here with Father. He might've found out something about your mother by then," he said, and Grace nodded.

"I'll see you then," she replied.

As he hurried off, Grace stood on the steps and watched him go. It had been quite a day, the discovery of the truth about her parents, and the discovery of the truth about Thomas's true feelings for her. Grace was not used to knowing the truth.

So much of it had been kept from her as she grew up. But in what had occurred today, she felt blessed and happy to allow events to play out as they would. Her life had been a series of twists and turns, believing things about herself, and discovering they were false.

She had known loss, and had mourned it, too. But until today, she had not known the real object of that loss, even as she could feel no real sense of loss at the thought of the professor's death. He was a detached figure, distant, but still her father, as was Lady Thornberry, her mother.

"It's all very confusing," she said to herself, even as she knew her feelings for Thomas were very real, and the family that really mattered was hers already.

LADY THORNBERRY

"*I*'ve found her!" Doctor Mullen exclaimed, bursting into the room as Grace and Thomas were waiting expectantly for luncheon to begin.

Grace stared at him in astonishment, and the doctor held up a piece of paper, waving it above his head in an excited frenzy.

"Lady Thornberry, Father? Have you really found her?" Thomas exclaimed, and Doctor Mullen placed the piece of paper ceremoniously in Grace's hands.

Her own were trembling, and she held it up, reading aloud the address.

"*Lady Lucy Thornberry, Apartment Two, Manor Heights Crescent, Mayfair, London,*" she read as Thomas rose excitably to his feet.

"Come along, let's go at once," he said, even as Doctor Mullen raised his hands.

"I'm not sure we should burst in on her unannounced. It might be better to wait," he said, but Grace could not contain herself.

She knew she had to see her, She had waited her whole life for this moment, even as she had not known it. The last time she had been in her mother's presence, she had been only six weeks old, departing with her father and governess for Newcastle.

Her heart was beating fast, and the thought of seeing her again, of hearing her voice...

"I don't think I *can* wait, Doctor Mullen. I need to see her. I've got to," Grace said, and Thomas nodded.

"Please, Father. We can go this afternoon. You can make the introduction. You knew the professor, and you can explain what we know to be true. She knows there was a shipwreck, that her husband died, and that she lost her child. But the rest... it'll need you to explain it..." he said, his words trailing off.

Grace, too, knew the difficulty in what they were proposing. There was no real evidence as to Grace's claim. The facts were as reported.

The ship had been wrecked, all hands had been lost, and Lady Thornberry had grieved for her dead husband and child. There was no reason for her to believe Grace *was* that child, and there may even have been others who had attempted to prove the lineage for themselves. But Grace wanted nothing from her mother, only the chance to see her, to speak to her, to make her understand... Doctor Mullen sighed.

"You're right, I suppose. There's no merit in waiting in any longer. We'd not achieve anything. To write would be futile. She'd dismiss the matter out of hand. No... we'll go. But we'll dine first. I've been out since breakfast, and I'm ravenous," he said.

The dishes for the luncheon had been set on the sideboard, and Thomas lifted one of the covers, making a face as he glanced back at Grace and his father.

"Oh, dear. It's devilled pig's kidney," he said, groaning as Grace hid her smile behind a napkin.

* * *

163

AFTER THEY HAD FINISHED LUNCHEON, Doctor Mullen summoned a hansom cab to take them to Mayfair and the home of Lady Thornberry.

Grace was feeling terribly nervous, and she was glad to have Thomas and Doctor Mullen at her side, the latter promising to explain the situation to Lady Thornberry in the hope of securing an interview with her. In truth, Grace did not know how she would be received.

She had grown used to loss and rejection, and if Lady Thornberry decided she wanted nothing to do with her, so be it. But to have returned to Norfolk without even so much as an attempt at reunion would have only caused her further heartache, and Grace she had to try, not for own sake, but that of Lady Thornberry, too.

"Isn't Mayfair a beautiful place?" Doctor Mullen said, as they drove past handsome townhouses and through neatly laid out squares with formal gardens at their centre, and fashionable men and women parading in the sunshine.

"It's a far cry from Carshalton," Thomas said, and Grace smiled.

"I'd have lived here, I suppose. But I doubt I'd have been permitted to learn anything about medicine," she replied.

Grace could well imagine the sort of life she would have led in such a place. Even with a father like Professor Thornberry, the chance of her learning anything about medicine would have been quite out of the question.

A governess would have taught her enough French to be polite, the rudiments of a music instrument, and how to paint a watercolour with detached accuracy. Her life would have been spent between drawing rooms and salons, taking tea and entertaining others who lived equally vacuous lives.

Never would she have been permitted to practise those things she took for granted now.

"You'd have lived a very different life, Grace, that's certainly true. But it doesn't mean you'd have found yourself unloved. I don't know much about what happened to Lady Thornberry after the shipwreck. She didn't remarry, I discovered that yesterday. But as for her heart... I've no doubt it was broken. I know what it's like to lose a spouse. But to do so in such tragic circumstances, and to lose a child, too. It's unimaginable," he said.

Grace nodded. She felt sorry for Lady Thornberry, who had lived with the pain of loss all these long years past. What would she say when she discovered the truth about her daughter? Would it make her happy?

There were so many unanswered questions, and as they pulled up outside the house, Grace could not help but feel terribly nervous as to what was to come. Thomas gave her a reassuring smile.

"It's all right. Father's going to explain everything to Lady Thornberry, then you can meet her for yourself," he said.

"If she agrees to it," Grace replied, for she still feared the possibility of rejection.

Her mother had no reason to believe her story, even as Doctor Mullen telling it would certainly add credibility. Thomas's father now climbed out of the carriage, making his way up the steps of the house and knocking at the large, imposing front door.

Grace and Thomas waited in the hansom cab, peering out nervously as Doctor Mullen was admitted by a servant.

"What will you say to her?" Thomas asked, but Grace shook her head.

She did not know what she would say, or even how to greet the woman she was to call mother. Lady Thornberry was a stranger, and yet she was no stranger at all. Their lives had been lived entirely separately, without even the recognition of one another's existence.

Lady Thornberry had assumed her daughter to be dead, and

Grace had never believed herself to have a mother, other than Mary Carruthers. Even when she had come to know the truth, Grace had hardly dared believe she would ever meet her real mother, even as she now waited to do just that.

But a sudden, terrible thought now struck, and she looked at Thomas in horror.

"What's wrong?" he asked.

"What if there's... a grave? What if she erected a memorial? I might've been... given a funeral," she said, astonished at the possibility of see her name, the name of Charlotte, carved on a memorial stone, the letters fading after all these years had passed.

But Thomas shook his head and slipped his hand into hers.

"You mustn't think like that, Grace. Besides, it doesn't matter, does it? I'm sure they *did* create a memorial. And I'm sure they grieved like any other family would grieve the loss of a child and its father. But you're alive, and that's all that matters," he said, smiling at Grace, who nodded.

At that moment, the door to the house was opened, and Doctor Mullen appeared, beckoning to Grace and Thomas as he did so.

"She wants to see you, Grace. You're to go into the drawing room, alone," he said.

Grace felt terribly nervous, but she nodded, glancing back at Thomas, who gave her a reassuring smile.

"We'll be waiting for you out here," he said, and Grace made her way up the steps, ushered into the house by an imperious-looking man, whom she assumed to be the butler.

"This way," he said, leading Grace through the hallway.

The house was comfortably furnished, the hallway in mahogany, with paintings of classical scenes lining the walls. A staircase led up to a landing above, and a large, ticking grandfather clock stood in the corner.

As they approached a door at the far end of the passageway

leading from the hallway, a loud yapping indicated the presence of a dog, and as the butler opened the door, a ball of white fur emerged, snapping at Grace's ankles, and causing her to cry out in alarm.

"Millicent, come here," a voice called from inside, and the dog obeyed, retreating into the drawing room, as Grace stood on the threshold.

She could not yet see the occupant of the room, the butler was standing in her way, and the door opened into the room. On a far wall, a portrait of a young woman immediately caught her eye.

It was the very image of Grace herself, brown haired and blue eyed, her cheeks rosy, her smile just as Grace's was lighting up her face.

"My lady, the girl to see you," the butler said.

"Show her in, Timpson," Lady Thornberry said, and the butler turned to Grace and indicated for her to enter the room.

As Grace did so, the dog barked, and she came face to face with a woman sitting in a chair by the hearth. She was around the same age as Doctor Mullen, dressed in black, her face pale, her lips red, and her hair tied back into a bun. As she looked Grace up and down, her eyes grew wide, and she glanced at the painting on the wall, its mirror image now standing before her.

"Good day, Lady Thornberry," Grace said, unsure of what to say or how to address her mother, who now rose to her feet, reaching out a trembling hand to touch Grace's cheek.

"I... I didn't ever expect. Oh, but... it can't be," she exclaimed, even as Grace smiled at her.

"Doctor Mullen explained the circumstances to you, didn't he?" she said, and Lady Thornberry nodded.

"He did, but... I didn't expect... oh, but it's you. I see myself in you. I can't believe it... after all these years. To think you were... lost, thought dead, and now..." she stammered, as tears rolled down her cheeks.

167

"I was taken in, Lady Thornberry, by the woman responsible for the shipwreck. She took care of me. I think she felt guilty for what had happened. And there was Lady Edith, too. They swore to take care of me. But I didn't... well, I didn't realize the truth, and I certainly didn't believe I'd ever find you," Grace replied.

She felt suddenly overwhelmed and sank into the chair opposite her mother's. Millicent barked, but Lady Thornberry shushed her, pulling her own chair close to Grace's and slipping her hands into hers.

"The portrait on the wall. It was painted when I was your age. I often look at it, and I used to wonder what you'd be like. I used to dream of seeing you again. When Doctor Mullen explained the circumstances, I thought... well, I thought you were just another liar. I've had them before, but... there's no mistaking you, Charlotte," she said.

Grace looked up at her and smiled, even as the tears rolled down her cheeks. It felt strange to be addressed as Charlotte, the name she had been given by the mother sitting before her. A name she had never used, and yet was her own.

"It was all by chance, you see," she said, and she explained what had happened at the medical school, and how she and Thomas had searched in the archives for the truth.

"And that led you to me. Your poor father... I used to picture him on the ship, holding you in his arms as it sank beneath the waves. He was a great man, the greatest doctor of our time. I'm still in mourning. One never truly recovers from such a loss. To lose one's dearest friend and companion, and the child they brought into the world, and yet..." Lady Thornberry said, her words trailing off, as she raised her hands to Grace's face, gazing into her eyes with such love as to bring tears to Grace's eyes, too.

"I'm here now, Mother," she whispered, and the two of them embraced.

It was the strangest of feelings for Grace, to see her very

image in her mother's portrait, and now to learn more about the man she would call her father. They had so much to discuss, and the butler brought them tea and cakes, as Lady Thornberry told Grace something of her life, and asked her questions about hers, too.

"But tell me, Grace, did you remain always in Carshalton? I don't understand your connection to Doctor Mullen. He talked of you as his ward," Lady Thornberry said.

To any outsider, Grace's life with both Doctor Berkley and Doctor Mullen must have appeared odd. Neither of them had coveted a ward, an assistant, a nurse, a friend, or whatever else Grace might be called in their company. But it was an arrangement bearing much fruit, and Grace knew how much she owed both these men for her happiness.

"After my... Mary died, I was taken care of by Lady Edith, another of the wreckers. I loved her dearly, though, and when she died, I was heartbroken. The village physician, Doctor Berkley, took me in, but he lost his life trying to rescue other unfortunate souls from a wrecked ship, and when Doctor Mullen arrived in Carshalton, I had nowhere else to go. I remained as his assistant. I've only ever wanted to be a nurse, you see," Grace replied.

She feared her mother would be horrified at such a revelation, but a smile came over her face, and she nodded.

"How wonderful. Your father always said nurses weren't appreciated properly . He believed in their profession and admired them for their diligence in caring for those in need, particularly the religious sisters who undertook such work. But tell me, Doctor Mullen said you'd learned a great deal, that you were as proficient in medical knowledge as any student at the medical school, including his son. You dress wounds, set bones, treat all manner of illnesses... it's quite remarkable," she said, and Grace blushed.

She felt proud to hear of Doctor Mullen's praise, and she

169

hoped the reunion with her mother would not spell the end of her work in medicine, but perhaps a new beginning.

"I've always wanted to be a nurse, ever since I saw Mary nursing Lady Edith. She did so with such tenderness and care. I know then I wanted to help others. But I've learned so much about medicine. First from Doctor Berkley, and then from Doctor Mullen. At a lecture the other day, with Doctor McKirahan, I knew an answer to a question none of the other medical students knew," Grace said, and her mother looked impressed.

"Then there's surely no more proof needed as to your being your father's daughter. He'd be proud of you, Charlotte, I... I'm sorry, I shouldn't call you Charlotte, should I? You're Grace, and that's how you're to be known," she said, but Grace shook her head.

She did not mind her mother calling her Charlotte. It was the name she herself had chosen for her, and whilst Grace was her familiar name, Charlotte was the name by which she should always have been known.

"I like them both. And I don't mind if you want to call me Charlotte. I'm just glad... to have found you," she said.

Grace had spent so much of her life wondering as to who she was and where she had come from. She had invented so many stories for herself, imagining this person or that person as her mother or father. But to know the truth, to be in her mother's presence, and to ask all the questions she had always wanted answers to, felt like a dream.

"And I'm so glad you found me, Grace. I've lived under a shadow for too long, but your coming home... it's brought light into the darkness. It took a long time for me to be able to think of you without bursting into tears. I blamed myself for not being there on the ship with you. I was suffering from a fever at the time, and your father insisted I take the train to Newcastle and meet you there. He was meant to call at Hull to take on medical supplies. If only he hadn't travelled by ship. But he loved the sea, and he'd journeyed to so many far-off places, he felt at home on the water," Lady Thornberry said, shaking her head sadly.

Grace took her mother's hand in hers and squeezed it. She hoped her presence was a comfort, and now they had so much to look forward to. She had quite lost track of time, and she was surprised to hear the clock on the mantelpiece strike four O'clock.

"Oh, Doctor Mullen and Thomas, they'll be waiting for me outside," she exclaimed, having been quite caught up in the reunion with her mother.

"Invite them in for tea. We can make a merry party, I'm sure. I'd like to meet Thomas. Has he been good to you?" Lady Thornberry asked, and Grace nodded.

"He's been very good to me. We're in love, you see. But don't tell Doctor Mullen. Thomas needs to finish his medical studies first," she said, and her mother smiled.

"A mother and daughter can share secrets, Grace," she said, tapping her nose.

Doctor Mullen and Thomas were duly invited to take tea, and after Millicent had calmed herself and was no longer yapping at their heals, the four of them were able to enjoy a pleasant conversation. Grace could still not believe her good fortune, and the chance discovery that had changed her life.

"But what do you intend to do now, Grace?" Doctor Mullen asked, as more tea and cake was brought by the butler.

Grace had not given the matter much consideration, if any. Her life had changed in an instant, and as the daughter of a woman like Lady Thornberry, many doors lay open to her. But despite these new opportunities, Grace knew she had unfinished business in Carshalton.

The wreckers were still at large, and knowing herself as their victim, too, Grace was determined to put a stop to their wicked work. But more so than that, Grace was not about to abandon her studies, or the many people she had helped over the years. She still wanted to be Doctor Mullen's assistant, and continue learning, as Doctor McKirahan had encouraged her to do.

"I'm not sure. But I know I want to come home with you. I'll be sad to leave, but... I don't want things to come to an end," she said, glancing at Thomas, who shook his head.

"I'm sure Father won't mind you doing so. And you can come to London anytime you wish," he said, and Doctor Mullen nodded.

"Certainly, you can. But what does Lady Thornberry think?" he asked.

Grace turned to her mother, who was stroking Millicent on her lap. She smiled at Grace and nodded.

"I can't expect you to abandon everything you've worked for, Grace. I want us to get to know one another, but I won't force you away from the things you hold dear. If you want to go back to Carshalton, you should go back to Carshalton. You have my blessing," she said, and Grace nodded.

She wanted both to stay and to go, to continue her work, and to know her mother better. But there was time for all of that, and in this moment, in the here and now, Grace was content to be surrounded by those who loved her, both now, and in the past.

"And we mustn't distract Thomas any longer from his studies," Doctor Mullen said, raising his eyebrows.

Thomas blushed, glancing at Grace, who smiled.

"He's going to make the finest of doctors," she said, and her mother smiled.

"And it seems you're going to make the finest of nurses, too, Grace," she said.

"I don't know about that..." Grace said, though she felt flattered by her mother's praise.

But Doctor Mullen shook his head.

"She's only being modest, Lady Thornberry. If it wasn't for

Grace, Carshalton would be all the poorer, as would I. I've come to depend on her entirely," he said.

Grace blushed. She was not used to such praise. Doctor Mullen was usually so reserved, and yet it seemed he wanted to make his feelings known to Lady Thornberry, and there was no doubting his pride in Grace's achievements.

"She's a remarkable young woman," Lady Thornberry said, and the others smiled.

"She certainly is, and I'm so glad she's discovered the truth as to who she is," Doctor Mullen replied.

THE WRECKER'S SCOURGE

race, Thomas, and Doctor Mullen remained in Lady Thornberry's company for the rest of the evening. The following day, and day after, Grace spent time with her mother, the two of them sharing a lifetime of memories.

The more they discovered about one another, the more, it seemed, they had in common. Grace and her mother were very much alike, not only in looks, but in mannerisms and interests, too.

Lady Thornberry played the piano, and Grace was reminded of the many times she had sat in the company of Lady Edith, listening to her play the piano, too.

"I wish I'd learned to play for myself," Grace said, watching as Lady Thornberry's fingers moved effortlessly across the keys.

"Why don't you try?" she said, rising from the piano stool and inviting Grace to sit down.

Grace smiled. She knew nothing about playing the piano, but sitting in front of the instrument, she felt a sense of familiarity, remembering the pleasure on Lady Edith's face as she played.

She struck a chord, then another, trying to recall the distant memory of a tune.

"It goes, dah, dah, dee, dah, dee, dah, dee, dee," she said, humming the notes, and Lady Thornberry leaned over her and played the precise tune with one hand.

Grace looked up at her in astonishment, marvelling at the ease with which her mother played.

"But... how did you know it?" Grace asked.

"It's a well-known song – *The Flight of the Butterfly*," she said, and she played the notes again, a simple melody, repeated, as though the butterfly itself was fluttering about the room.

Grace was in awe, and she was reminded of the possibility of what her life might have been like had she not been separated from her parents. She, too, would have learned to play the piano, just like her mother.

She would have entertained visitors – suitors, too. There was a whole other life here, one she had missed out on, even as she did not regret the way things had now turned out.

She had her life, and her mother had hers. They were different yet brought together by circumstance. It was a strange feeling, one Grace was still getting used to.

"I suppose I could learn to play it. But... we don't have a piano in Carshalton," Grace said, and her mother smiled.

"You could stay here and learn," she said, sitting down at the piano stool next to Grace.

Grace sighed. She had been convinced as to the thought of returning to Norfolk, but the more time she spent with her mother, the more she felt torn between two worlds. There was so much she still wanted to know. Her mother had told her of cousins and aunts she was to meet, and places they would go together – a whole world was opening before her, and yet she felt torn between *it* and her past.

"But I... oh, I don't know. I promised Doctor Mullen... he's been so good to me. And then... there're the wreckers, too," Grace said.

Her mother looked at her fearfully.

"Grace... I don't want you to put yourself in danger. These wreckers... the things you've told me... why not forget about it all? Come back home," she said, but Grace shook her head.

"I heard the cries of the men in the water that night. There was no hope for any of them. Doctor Berkley died a hero, but he died needlessly, too. There should never have been a shipwreck – *The Honoria,* nor the one we tried to prevent, either. Countless lives lost... I've tried so hard, but I've never... well, I can't let it rest," she said, and her mother nodded and put her arm around her.

"But you'll come back, won't you? I've just found you, and... I can't bear the thought of you leaving me again," she said, and tears welled up in her eyes.

"I promise, Mother – I promise I'll come back," Grace replied, and it was a promise she intended to keep.

Grace had made a promise to the memory of Doctor Berkley. He had been her friend when no one else had been, and she knew she could not live with herself whilst those responsible for his death, and so many other deaths, too, including her father's, remained free.

Mrs. Parks, Captain Dickinson, the other servants, the curate, Mrs. Wilks... all of them had a hand in it, and Grace was sworn to see justice done.

* * *

"DON'T FORGET THE DIFFERENCE – if you set the leg the wrong way, well... it'll heal the wrong way," Grace said, as she bid Thomas goodbye.

He grinned at her.

"I'll try to remember the difference – left and right, that sort of thing. But how am I going to manage without you?" he asked.

Grace smiled. It was the morning of her departure from London to Norfolk with Doctor Mullen. They had been away from Carshalton for two weeks, and yet it seemed as though a lifetime had passed.

She had discovered so much, about herself and her feelings, about her past and her future. It was astonishing, and even now, Grace felt torn between one world and another. But her mind was made up, and until the wreckers were brought to justice, her place was in Carshalton.

"You'll manage – you've got a whole library full of books to study from," Grace said, but Thomas shook his head.

"But that means nothing – it's how to use the knowledge that counts. You're the one who taught me that," he said, and Grace put her arms around him and sighed.

"I'll see you very soon. It won't be long before the examinations are over and you can come home," she said.

At that moment, the door to their lodgings opened, and Doctor Mullen appeared. He looked surprised to see the two of them embrace, but said nothing, merely giving the hint of a smile, as he directed the maid to bring out their bags. Lady Thornberry's carriage had just drawn up, and she was to take them to the station for their journey onto Norwich.

"Goodbye, Thomas. Work hard, and we'll see you soon," Doctor Mullen said, shaking Thomas by the hand.

Unexpected tears rose in Grace's eyes. Not only was she leaving her mother behind, but Thomas, too. She would miss him dreadfully, even as the two of them had promised to write each week and assured one another of their love and fidelity.

"I'll miss you," Thomas said, slipping his hand into Grace's and squeezing it.

"I'll miss you, too. I'll write when I have news," Grace said, and Thomas nodded.

"Be careful, Grace," he replied.

The driver of Lady Thornberry's carriage opened the compartment door for them, and as they climbed in beside her, she smiled at Grace, glancing out of the window at Thomas, who now came to run by the side of the carriage set off.

"Parting can be such sweet sorrow," she said as Grace fought back the tears.

She had not expected to feel like this, but things had changed between her and Thomas, and they had come to realize feelings they had not shared before. No longer was this only a parting of friends, but of love, too.

"You'll see one another soon," Doctor Mullen said, smiling at Grace, and it was as though he knew the truth as to how they felt about one another, and was sympathetic to a possible future between them.

Grace pulled out a handkerchief and dabbed her eyes.

"I'll be all right," she said, smiling at Lady Thornberry, who took her hand in hers and squeezed it.

"I hope you'll return very soon, Grace. I'll miss you terribly. I might even come to Norfolk myself, though… I wonder how I'd feel. I'd never heard of Carshalton, until… well, the shipwreck. I vowed never to see it, and yet… I'd like to. They never found his body, you see. It's foolish, but these last few days, I've imagined him walking through the drawing room door, just as you did," she said.

Grace smiled at her mother. She could understand the pain of loss. It was the same pain she had known at the loss of Mary Carruthers, of Lady Edith, and of Doctor Berkley. Grace knew what it was to mourn, and now she feared she was causing Lady Thornberry fresh upset in leaving.

"I wish he would," Grace said, and her mother sighed.

"So do I. But I've got you, haven't I. And I know I'll see you come back very soon," Lady Thornberry said.

Grace promised she would, but as they said goodbye to Lady

Thornberry at the station, Grace knew she could not return until matters with the wreckers were settled. She knew the truth now – the truth about her father and the life she would have lived, had it not been for the cruel actions of those responsible for the wrecking of *The Honoria*.

How many other lives had been destroyed by their actions – those who had lost loved ones and livelihoods?

"I'll write to you," Grace said, as her mother kissed her and held her in her embrace on the platform.

"And I'll write to you, too. Goodbye, Grace – Charlotte," she said, and Grace looked up at her and smiled.

She would always be Grace, and yet she was so glad to have found herself known as Charlotte, too.

* * *

"FIRST CLASS, HOW SPLENDID," Doctor Mullen said, shutting the door of their compartment as the train gave a final whistle before pulling out of the station.

Lady Thornberry had paid for their tickets and given Grace the promise of a modest allowance in the months to come.

"Once you decide what to do next, we can discuss matters further," she had said, promising Grace a bright future.

"It was very kind of her to pay the fare for us," Grace replied, sitting opposite Doctor Mullen, who smiled at her.

"It's been quite an eventful two weeks, hasn't it?" he said, and Grace smiled.

"You could say that. But I owe it all to you, Doctor Mullen. I'm so grateful to you," she said, but Doctor Mullen shook his head.

"It was you and Thomas who discovered the truth about your father. I only helped join the pieces together," he said, blushing as Grace reached out to take his hand in hers.

"But I'm really so grateful, Doctor Mullen. I hope you know that. Whatever happens, I'll always be grateful to you," she said.

Doctor Mullen smiled.

"Dear me, you'll have me growing sentimental, Grace. But… you've been like a daughter to me, and I'm so glad… well, I'm so happy to think you and Thomas… forgive me… I couldn't help but realise it," he said, and now it was Grace's turn to blush.

"We've grown close over the years. He's going to ask me to marry him – when he's finished his studies, of course, and with your blessing," Grace said, and Doctor Mullen nodded.

"You have my blessing, Grace – both of you. I just hope he manages with his examinations. It's one thing to be top of the class, but quite another to excel in the examination hall. I hope he's diligent in his studies, like you," he said.

But Grace had every confidence in Thomas's abilities, and as they sped through the Norfolk countryside on the steam train, she thought of all the wonderful possibilities lying ahead. She and Thomas had talked a great deal about the future – about their plans for a medical practice, and the possibility of new and exciting discoveries.

"I think he'll make a fine doctor," she said, looking up from the book she was reading.

It was a volume on contagious diseases, one Thomas had leant her to study from. Doctor Mullen smiled.

"You're right, Grace – but he can be too headstrong and sure of himself. I fear they won't like that in the examinations. They want the answer, that's all. I wonder… do you ever imagine yourself taking such examinations? If only it was possible," Doctor Mullen said.

Grace had thought a great deal about such questions since seeing the medical school and attending Doctor McKirahan's lecture. She would dearly have loved to sit in on the examinations, but she knew it was not possible.

She could study every medical textbook ever written, and

still be barred from even an attempt. The fact of who her father was would make no difference. Women did not become doctors, and that was final.

"I imagine it, yes, but I don't think I could do so. It wouldn't be allowed, would it?" she and Doctor Mullen shook his head.

"No, but... perhaps there might be a way of cheating the system. If Doctor McKirahan was willing, perhaps you could sit the examinations in secret. You'd not receive any qualification, of course, but you'd know you'd reached the standard. I've no doubt you'd excel at such a task," Doctor Mullen said.

The thought was an intriguing one, even as Grace could think of a dozen reasons not to agree. She did not want to be second to the others – an object of pity and charity. If she was to pass the examinations, she wanted to do so publicly, so that everyone could see.

"Couldn't I take them in memory of my father?" she asked, and Doctor Mullen nodded.

"Perhaps... I'll write to Doctor McKirahan, and your mother would still have influence, of course," he said.

Grace did not know whether her mother would approve of her sitting the examinations. Lady Thornberry had been impressed to hear of Grace's diligence in her studies and of her desire to be a nurse, but it had seemed to Grace as though her mother was also of the opinion she should step back from such pursuits, now she had the assurance of a stable future ahead of her.

"It's not usual for young ladies to take up the task of nursing," Lady Thornberry had said, even as Grace had made clear her intentions.

"I'd like to try, at least," Grace said, and Doctor Mullen promised to write to Doctor McKirahan and see what might be done.

They arrived at Norwich on time, and were helped with their bags by the stewards to a waiting carriage. It would take them as far as the ravine above Carshalton, where a horse and trap from one of the arms could take them the rest of the way.

"I wonder what we've missed whilst we've been away," Doctor Mullen said, as they drove across the fens in the carriage.

Grace smiled. There would be a list of ailments for them to attend to: complaints of the stomach, dislocated joints, broken bones, headaches and nausea... she was looking forward to returning home, even as she no longer felt Carshalton to be the only home she had. But there was a more pressing matter, too – more so than the treating ailments or worrying about medical examinations.

Grace knew she could not rest until the wreckers were brought to justice. They had killed her father and had killed the man she had looked up to as a father, too. Now was the time to a put a stop to their wicked activities, and when the next storm came, Grace would be ready...

THE CREARY CAVE

*A*s Grace had predicted, she and Doctor Mullen dealt with a steady stream of ailments in the days following their return to Carshalton, setting off on their rounds early on the following morning.

The Bartlett sisters had been in bed for a week with a fever, and Clara Dickson had her arm in a makeshift sling, having pulled the muscles milking her dairy herd. Joseph Peggetty's son, Arthur, had boils on his feet, and the landlord of the village inn was complaining of short-sightedness.

Grace and Doctor Mullen treated each of them with due care and attention, and soon enough they had caught up with the backlog of patients, several of whom complained as to their absence.

"I thought I was dying, and where was the doctor? In London, of all places," Lilian Bartlett said, as Doctor Mullen held the thermometer under her tongue.

"It's rare for me to be away, Miss Bartlett, but I was visiting my son. He's at medical school, as you know. Grace came with me. But I'm back now, and I can confirm you're not going to die. Not yet, anyway," he said, glancing at Grace, who smiled.

Miss Bartlett, a formidable figure in village life, narrowed her eyes. She was lying in bed, the blankets pulled up over her, and with her sister asleep at her side.

"We've had some strange things going on here," he said, and Doctor Mullen looked at her with interest.

"What sort of things?" he said, and Miss Bartlett beckoned him closer, as though fearful of being overheard by some unseen presence.

"Flashing lights, Doctor Mullen. I saw them last night, and the night before, and the night before that. They were coming from Howard's Hill, where that old Wicks woman lives. I wouldn't have seen them if I hadn't been confined to bed. Usually, I stay up reading until late, as does my sister. But we both saw it — flashing lights. There was a terrible storm two nights ago, and I thought there'd be one last night, too. You hear tell of the wreckers, but..." she said, her words trailing off.

"That's very interesting, Miss Bartlett. I wonder..." Doctor Mullen replied, glancing at Grace, who was gripped by a sudden fear.

It was another plot to wreck a ship. She had heard low rumbles of thunder the night before, but only a few spots of rain had fallen, and the night had remained calm and sultry. But the lights shining from Howard's Hill were proof of what was being planned, and when Grace and Doctor Mullen had left the home of the Bartlett sisters, Grace was anxious to do something to prevent another tragedy.

"It's the same pattern–the light from Mrs. Wicks' cottage, signalling to Captain Dickinson and the others at Carshalton House," she said, and Doctor Mullen nodded.

"And look at the weather. It's closing in. A storm's going to break," Doctor Mullen said, as they made their way down the ravine towards the village.

Grace's heart was beating fast. She had not expected the

opportunity to come so soon, but now was their chance, and if they did not act now, they might not have an opportunity again.

Her mind was racing, and she thought back to the times they had seen the lights flash out from the headland. It was always the same place, where they had seen the footmarks in the sand, and a sudden thought now occurred to her.

"We need to find a way up the cliff. We can't catch them by going along the headland–they'd scatter. But if we came on them by surprise..." she said, and Doctor Mullen nodded.

"But the two of us can't do it alone. They outnumber us, and what about the rest of the village?" he said.

Grace thought for a moment. Doctor Mullen was right. They did not know who might betray them, but there was one person she felt certain they could trust. The landlord who had come to Doctor Berkley's aid, and the other men who had so bravely manned the lifeboats.

"The landlord," Grace said, and Doctor Mullen nodded.

"I'll go and talk to him. You find a way up the cliff. But be careful. The rocks can be treacherous, but you know that well enough," he said.

Grace nodded. This was it. This was the moment she had been waiting for, and she hurried off in the direction of the beach, even as a low rumble of thunder echoed above the ravine.

The tide was on the turn, the waves breaking gently on the sand. To an observer unfamiliar with the sea, they might think the waters were calm and placid. But when the storm came, the waves would be whipped up into a frenzy, crashing on the rocks, and bringing devastation to any boat attracted by the lights.

Grace hurried along the sand, gazing up at the cliffs above, where the headland jutted out towards the sea. She began to climb, picking her way over the rocks, and tracing a route upwards. She had done it many times before, searching for seagull eggs or gathering plants that only grew on the cliffs. But as she came to a jut in the rock, she was surprised to hear voices echoing from below.

There was a cave there, known locally as Creary Cave, a crevice carved deep into the rock by the gradual erosion of the waves. Peering over the precipice, Grace caught sight of the top of several heads at the entrance to the cave, leaning forward in discussion.

"Tonight, there's a ship called *The Golden Arrow*. It's a cargo ship, laden with all manner of goods. The storm's coming. We don't need Mrs. Wicks to signal. We can wait on the headland ourselves. We'll see it, won't we?" one of them was saying.

Grace knew the speaker without seeing his face. It was Captain Dickinson, and the other voices, too, were readily discernible. Mrs. Parks, Dolby Cleverley, the curate... they were all there, and they plotting the wrecking of another innocent ship.

It made Grace so angry to hear these words, and she imagined the same scene eighteen years previously, as *The Honoria* sailed to its doom.

"And what if someone gets suspicious? That fool, Wicks, keeps flashing the light from her cottage. She knows to wait until she sights a ship–not just hears a rumble of thunder," Mrs. Parks said.

"We'll deal with her later. But for now, we'll stay here and wait. Understood?" Captain Dickinson said, and the others murmured their agreement.

Grace stayed listening for a while, knowing there was no time to warn Doctor Mullen of what she had heard, and she could only hope the landlord had agreed to help them. As dusk fell, the wreckers lit a fire at the entrance to the cave, laughing and joking with one another as to the spoils to come.

"*The Golden Arrow*–one can just imagine its cargo," Captain Dickinson said.

"I hope I find some jewellery washed up tomorrow morning, or something I can sell–a pocket watch or a compass. I sold the ship's compass from *The Honoria*," Mrs. Parks boasted.

At the mention of the Honoria, Grace leaned over the parapet to listen, spluttering as the smoke from the fire stung her eyes.

"That was the boat they took the baby from, wasn't it? Grace Carruthers," Captain Dickinson replied.

"That's right. If only she'd drowned along with the rest of them. She'd have saved us all a lot of trouble," Mrs. Parks replied, and the others laughed.

Grace would gladly have leaped on the wicked housekeeper there and then, but now she bided her time, all the more determined to do whatever it took to put a stop to them, and as darkness fell, the sound of a foghorn was heard in the distance...

* * *

"COME ALONG, Mrs. Parks, we don't have long. Take my hand," Captain Dickinson said.

Grace was hiding by the jut in the rock, watching the figures of the wreckers climbing up the cliff. They had a lantern with them, and as the ship's horn sounded in the distance, Grace knew it would not be long before the flashing began, and *The Golden Arrow* was lured onto the rocks.

"I'm coming, it's just... oh," Mrs. Parks cried.

There was the sound of stones falling from the cliff, and a clamour of voices. For a moment, Grace wondered if the housekeeper had fallen, but the voice of Captain Dickinson now rang out.

"I've got you, Mrs. Parks, keep hold of my hand," he said, and the party now continued its way up the cliff.

Grace was following from a distance, intending to hide close to the top, before confronting the wreckers at the arrival of

Doctor Mullen and the landlord. She could only hope they would come in force and the wreckers could be brought to justice.

They had reached the top of the cliff now, and the foghorn sounded again out to sea, as a rumble of thunder echoed above. Lightning lit up the scene, and Grace ducked to hide behind a large rock, not wanting to be seen behind the others. The wind was picking up, and the rain was beginning to fall.

"Excellent wrecking weather," the curate called out, and the others laughed.

It disgusted Grace to hear the callous way they talked, as though the prospect of so many lives lost meant nothing to them. She could imagine their cries of delight at the spoils on the beach the following morning, caring nothing for the bodies washed up in the surf.

It made her shudder to think of it, and angry at the memory of so many lives lost at the hands of these wicked men and women. It had surely been a night just like this when *The Honoria* had been lost, and she pictured her father on the deck, holding her in his arms, and watching as the captain fought bravely against the elements.

"Flash the light, Mrs. Parks–it'll be close enough by now," Captain Dickinson said, and the light appeared above, and illuminating the scene like a flash of lightning.

There were five wreckers there–Captain Dickinson, Mrs. Parks, Dolby, the curate, and a man whom Grace did not recognise. He was strongly built, his face obscured by a large hat pulled down over his eyes. He wore a sou'wester, and was pointing out to sea, where another light now appeared.

"They've seen us," he said, and the others laughed.

"And now they'll think they're coming into safe harbour in a storm," the curate said, rubbing his hands together gleefully.

"Think of all the tobacco, the brandy…" Dolby said, and the

five of them were worked up into a frenzy of possibility as to what might be theirs.

Grace was still hiding below the cliff edge, longing for the sound of footsteps and the shout of Doctor Mullen and the landlord.

"What if they don't come?" she said to herself, fearing it would be too late to prevent disaster.

"Flash more rapidly, Mrs. Parks, lure them in," Captain Dickinson said, and the light flashed even brighter.

Grace could not bear it any longer. She felt so angry, and now she emerged from below the cliff edge, charging towards Mrs. Parks with a cry.

The housekeeper was taken by surprise, and Grace knocked the lamp from her hands. It fell onto the rocks and smashed, plunging them into darkness. Mrs. Parks let out an angry cry, grabbing at Grace, who knocked her to the ground.

The curate, too, grabbed hold of Grace, whilst Dolby and the other man scrambled to find the lamp.

"Get it lit again," Captain Dickinson cried, as Grace rolled on the ground with Mrs. Parks.

"You wicked child," the housekeeper cried, but Grace struck her hard across the face, the anger of the years welling up inside her.

Mrs. Parks screamed, and Grace wrenched free from her grip, knocking the curate backwards with a cry. He, too, fell to the ground, and Grace turned, about to flee, when strong arms grabbed her from behind. It was Captain Dickinson, and now he held her in an iron grip.

"You little wretch–following us, I suppose. I should toss you off the cliff. How dare you," he snarled, as Grace struggled in his arms.

"Let me go," she cried, and now she screamed, her voice echoing through the driving wind, as a sudden shout came from along the headland.

The sou'wester clad man and Dolby had managed to relight the lamp, and were flashing it out to sea, the ship's foghorn sounding in the distance. But as Grace struggled in Captain Dickinson's arms, she saw a welcome sight approaching–figures running along the headland, at least a dozen, and led by Doctor Mullen, who called out to her through the wind and rain.

"Grace, are you there?" he called out.

"I'm here, Doctor Mullen," she shouted back, even as Captain Dickinson pulled her towards the cliff edge.

Mrs. Parks had staggered to her feet, and she grabbed hold of Grace by the collar, striking her across the face.

"Little wretch," she snarled, but Grace was not afraid of her, and lashing out, she kicked the housekeeper hard in the shin, causing her to fall back in pain.

As she did so, Captain Dickinson stumbled, and his grip on Grace loosened, she turned, pushing against him with all her might, and now he fell, letting out a cry, as he tumbled over the cliff edge. Grace fell back, caught in the arms of Doctor Mullen, who pulled her back to safety.

"My darling, Grace, my poor child... oh, are you all right?" he exclaimed, holding her in his arms.

Grace looked up at him and smiled.

"I stopped them, Doctor Mullen," she said, and the doctor nodded.

"You did, Grace," he said, glancing over his shoulder to where the landlord and the other men had the sou'wester clad man and Dolby in their custody.

The lamp had been smashed, and the sound of *The Golden Arrow's* foghorn now echoed over the headland as though in thanks.

"It's steering away," one of the men called out, and Grace and Doctor Mullen breathed a sigh of relief.

The curate was still lying dazed on the ground, and Mrs. Parks was nursing a wound to her leg. Doctor Mullen approached the cliff edge warily.

"I can't see anything, but... it's a sheer drop from here," he said, as the waves crashed on the rocks below.

Grace shuddered. There was nothing she could have done to prevent Captain Dickinson from falling. He would have pulled her over with him. The landlord called out, peering over the drop, his hands cupped to his mouth.

"Captain Dickinson, can you hear me?" he shouted, but no reply came.

Dolby and the sou'wester clad man were now subdued, and the curate was hauled to his feet, muttering in confusion.

"My goodness, what a to do, I don't understand," he said, and to Grace's surprise, Doctor Mullen grabbed him by his collar.

"You'll understand this, curate. Tomorrow morning, I'll be writing to the Bishop, and you'll soon find yourself defrocked and without a living. You're a disgrace to the clerical state," he said, turning angrily, as the curate let out an exclamation.

"How dare you speak to me like that," he said, but no one was paying him any attention.

The threat of the magistrate had silenced Dolby, and the sou'wester clad man, who was still refusing to give his name. Grace turned to Mrs. Parks, who eyed her warily in the light of a small lantern held by one of the rescuers.

"And what of you, Mrs. Parks? What have you got to say for yourself?" Grace asked.

The housekeeper snarled at her.

"I did the same as your mother. She was just as bad. She was worse, in fact. It was her who started it. She came here full of stories about wrecking ships... and I doubt the apple falls far from the tree," she said.

But Grace shook her head. In saving *The Golden Arrow*, Grace had assuaged her guilt. Her mother was not Mary Carruthers. Her mother was Lady Thornberry, and her father was one of the many victims of Mrs. Parks and the others. This was the end of it. Justice was to be served and no ship need fear the light of the wreckers any longer.

"But she's not my mother. I know who my mother is. She's Lady Lucy Thornberry, and my father was Professor Sir Anstruther Thornberry, one of the greatest doctors to ever live. I should've lived a very different life, but I'm glad of the life I've had, and I'm glad it's brought me here now to put a stop to your wickedness and those of the others. I'm not afraid of you, Mrs. Parks, and I know I could never be like you. A doctor swears to save life, not take it, and that's a promise I've made, too," Grace replied, fixing the housekeeper with a defiant look.

Mrs. Parks had no words of retort, and the landlord now took her by the arm.

"We'll keep them in the inn overnight–keep a watch and guard. The constabulary can be sent for in the morning, one the storm's cleared," he said.

"You can't do that. I have the living of this parish, the cure of souls," the curate exclaimed.

"And what about the souls of those men at sea, curate? What will the almighty say when you stand before the judgement throne? I'm sure your cure of souls won't matter much then," Doctor Mullen said, shaking his head as the curate and the others were led away.

He and Grace were left standing above the cliffs. The rain had turned to a persistent drizzle, and the wind was dying down, the thunder now rumbling in the distance, the storm moving on.

Doctor Mullen put his arm around her. She was soaked to the skin and shivering, her hands and legs cut and bruised from the fall and struggle.

"We did it, Doctor Mullen – we saved the ship, and exposed the wreckers. But... do you think he's dead?" Grace asked, glancing towards the cliff edge.

Doctor Mullen nodded.

"I think so, yes – but he'd have had no qualms in seeing those poor men sent to their deaths, either. Perhaps there's justice in that," he said, and Grace nodded.

She would shed no tears for Captain Dickinson, and now they made their way home, shivering in their damp clothes, but thankful the ordeal was over.

As she sat by the fire in her nightgown, Doctor Mullen gently bathed her wounds, and Grace thought back to all that had happened on that fateful night.

"What's going to happen to them? Mrs. Parks and the others, I mean?" Grace asked.

Doctor Mullen looked up at her with a ponderous look on his face.

"It rather depends on the judge, I suppose. They were trying to wreck *The Golden Arrow*. We caught them in the act, and we'll all testify accordingly. But it'll be far harder to prove they were involved with the previous wrecks. Impossible, even. We can only hope justice is served," he said, and Grace nodded.

She thought of Captain Dickinson, knowing justice had been served on him, even if no one else.

"And what about Carshalton House? If he's dead, I wonder who it goes to. He never married, and there can't be an heir," she said, pondering the matter, as Doctor Mullen cleared away the bloodied bandages and washed his hands.

"Those are questions for the morning, Grace. For now, let's be grateful for what's been done tonight, and leave the rest to the future," he said.

Grace nodded, thinking of Thomas and Lady Thornberry, and of all she had to tell them. She was exhausted, and as she lay down to sleep that night, she felt thankful it was all over.

"*But what comes next?*" she wondered, even as she knew she had done the right thing, and justice had been served.

THE EXAMINATION

*T*he arrival of the constabulary to Carshalton brought with it considerable consternation. Not only were Mrs. Parks, Dolby, the curate, and the sou'wester clad men, whose name turned out to be Archibald Sheen, a resident of a nearby farm, implicated in the wrecking, but many others, too.

Mrs. Parks had wasted no time in naming others involved, including Mrs. Wicks, who was hauled unceremoniously from her bed and charged with aiding and abetting murder. She protested vehemently, as did so many others. But little by little, further evidence came to light.

Stolen goods were found in barns and outhouses, along with evidence of the ships they had come from, and little by little, a picture emerged of an entire community caught up in the wicked works of the wreckers.

Grace and Doctor Mullen assisted with the investigations, and their evidence, gathered over many years of visiting the homes of the sick and feeble, proved crucial in securing convictions. It was six weeks later, and Grace and Doctor Mullen had returned to their work of caring for the sick of the village.

"Half the village was involved, and the other half knew it was happening," Doctor Mullen said, shaking his head.

The whole thing was extraordinary, and Grace wrote dozens of letters to Thomas and Lady Thornberry, explaining the dramatic unfolding of events in the village.

"But there was just no way of stopping it," Grace replied, shaking her head sadly.

"With Captain Dickinson dead, that's the end of it," Doctor Mullen said, looking up from his desk.

The captain's body had been discovered on the beach the next day. He had not survived the fall.

The servants had left Carshalton House, fleeing before they could be implicated, and it now stood empty, its windows shuttered and forlorn. The captain had been buried next to Lady Edith, but few had come to mourn. The new curate, the previous now imprisoned for his crimes, had spoken only of an "unwelcome legacy."

"I hope it's the end of it," Grace said, even as she feared there could still be those who took the chance of flashing a light out to sea whenever a storm was brewing.

"There'll always be those who seek their own advantage at the expense of others, whether it be by wrecking or some other means. But not here, perhaps," Doctor Mullen said, just a knock came at the cottage door.

Grace went to answer it, and she was surprised to find Horace Fletcher, Lady Edith's solicitor, standing on the step. He had aged some years since last she had seen him, but his appearance was unmistakable, and he smiled at Grace, taking off his hat and nodding.

"Ah, Miss Carruthers. It's you I've come to see," he said, and Grace stepped aside to let him in.

Doctor Mullen rose to greet him, and the solicitor was offered a chair by the hearth. Grace made tea, curious as to why Mr. Fletcher should be visiting her.

"Have you come all the way from London just to see me, Mr. Fletcher?" Grace asked, serving the solicitor his tea.

"I have, yes, Grace. It's a matter of great importance. I think you're going to be rather surprised. Sit down, if you will," Mr. Fletcher said, and Grace sat down opposite him, looking at him curiously.

"Is it to do with Lady Edith?" Grace asked, and the solicitor nodded.

"That's right and Captain Dickinson, too. When Lady Edith died, she left you an allowance, as you know. Captain Dickinson did all he could to block the process, and thus you've received nothing to date. My hands were tied in the matter, but with his death, there's no legal reason to prevent your receiving the sum owed to you," Mr. Fletcher replied.

Grace felt pleased. Her opinion of Lady Edith was greatly reduced, but the money would be of great help to her, even as Lady Thornberry, too, had promised her an allowance.

"That's marvellous news, isn't it, Grace?" Doctor Mullen said, and Grace nodded.

"Ah, but there's more to it than that. Captain Dickinson had no heir. Presumably he believed he'd live a full and long life, and marry in due course, too. But his untimely death left a question as to inheritance. Carshalton House was his by rights following Lady Edith's death. But you, Grace, were her ward, and thus you're the sole inheritor of the estate," Mr. Fletcher said, smiling at Grace, whose eyes now grew wide with astonishment.

She could not believe what she was hearing, even as the solicitor now produced papers to prove his words. Grace was Lady Edith's sole heir.

Carshalton House was hers, along with the income from the village rents. She had become wealthier than she could ever have imagined, and she stared at the solicitor in disbelief.

"But I... it can't be," she said.

"But it is, Grace. It's all here, clear to see," Mr. Fletcher said, showing her the deeds to the estate.

Doctor Mullen smiled.

"What a turn up, Grace. I'm so pleased for you," he said, and tears rolled down Grace's cheeks.

It was astonishing, and the more she thought about it, the more she could not believe her good fortune. A sudden thought occurred to her, and she looked from Doctor Mullen to the solicitor, a smile breaking over her face.

"I wouldn't have to use it as a house, would I? It could become a hospital. Thomas and I could make it into a hospital, the finest in the land," she exclaimed, her mind now filled with possibility as to what she and Thomas could do.

Mr. Fletcher nodded.

"It's yours to do with as you please, Grace. If you want to turn the house into a hospital, so be it," he said, and Grace clapped her hands together in delight.

"Can you imagine it, Doctor Mullen? Our own hospital. A place of convalescence by the sea. I've got to write to Thomas and Lady Thornberry at once," she exclaimed, leaping to her feet, filled with excitement at the possibility of what was to come.

Mr. Fletcher, too, rose to his feet.

"You can take possession of the house at once. It'll need opening up and airing, I'm sure. But the rents might take a little longer to come in. It's been an interesting time in Carshalton lately, hasn't it? I read about it in the papers," he said, and Grace and Doctor Mullen exchanged glances.

"Quite a time, yes. But... over now, thank goodness, and thanks in no small part to Grace," Doctor Mullen replied.

The solicitor bid them good day, and after he had left, Grace wrote long letters to both Thomas and Lady Thornberry, telling them of her good news and outlining her plans for Carshalton House.

She intended to make it both a place of convalescence and research, where she and Thomas could welcome those most in need and seek cures for those illnesses still so perplexing to medicine.

"And we can name it The Doctor Berkley Memorial Hospital," she wrote, wanting some way to commemorate the man from whom she had learned so much, and from whom her inspiration had come.

"And will you work at the hospital, Doctor Mullen?" Grace asked, as she and the doctor set off on their rounds that afternoon.

"I hope I'll be welcome there. You and Thomas have such new-fangled ideas. Will you want one of the old guard breathing down your necks?" he asked.

Grace smiled and slipped her hand into his.

"Without you, I'd be nothing. I owe you so much. I couldn't imagine the hospital without you," she said, and Doctor Mullen smiled.

"Then I'd be delighted, Grace," he replied.

A LETTER ARRIVED from Thomas two days later. He was very excited about Grace's news, but wrote to say he was worried about his examinations, even as he had worked hard to study for them.

In the excitement of the wreckers being brought to justice, Grace had given little thought to the possibility of taking the examinations herself, but with the good fortune she now enjoyed, the thought of doing so returned.

"I want to go to London and see Thomas. I want to take the medical examinations, too," Grace told Doctor Mullen a few days later.

The doctor, too, had forgotten his promise, but he now sat

down to write to Doctor McKirahan, recommending Grace be given the same examination as the other medical students, though without the promise of a degree at the end.

"It'll only be for your own satisfaction," he warned, but Grace was content with that, even as she would dearly have loved to be a doctor in her own right.

"I just want to see if I can do it, that's all. I just want a chance to prove myself," she said, and a few days later, she was travelling in a first-class compartment towards London, intent on seeing Thomas and Lady Thornberry and sitting the examinations for herself.

"*Clavicle, Humerus, Femur, Sacrum, Tibia... oh, I'll never remember them all*," Grace said to herself, closing the textbook with a sigh.

Anatomy had never been her strongest subject. She was used to the practical side of medicine, and whilst she knew how to mend any broken bone, remembering their names was something different.

Doctor McKirahan had written to Doctor Mullen expressing his delight in the thought of Grace sitting the examinations but reminding him there could be no awarding of a degree at the end.

Grace was *not* a medical student, but if she could pass the examinations, Doctor McKirahan would ensure she was recognised in one way or another, if only by the faculty.

"We're coming into London now, Miss Carruthers," the steward said, opening the door of Grace's first-class compartment.

It felt strange to travel in such luxury, and as she alighted on the platform, Thomas was waiting to greet her. He rushed to embrace her, and she flung her arms around him, overjoyed to see him, and realising just how much she had missed him.

"What changes you've wrought, and what changes you've

experienced," he exclaimed, still holding her in his arms, as she smiled at him.

"It's quite astonishing, isn't it? Can you believe it? It's ours–Carshalton House–and when you pass your examinations, we'll turn it into a hospital," she said, as he slipped his hand into hers, and they made their way along the platform, where the engine stood steaming, and porters dashed back and forth with trunks and trolley.

Thomas looked at Grace with an anxious expression on his face.

"I... well, yes, *if* I pass," he said, and Grace looked at him in surprise.

"What do you mean? You're the best the student in the medical school. You're bound to pass," she exclaimed, but Thomas shook his head.

"I've fallen behind with my studies. I don't know... it's just not... easy," he said, and he explained to her he had been struggling with the workload.

The final examinations were to take place in the coming days. Papers on tropical diseases, anatomy, surgery, infection, and all manner of other medical topics were to be sat one after the other.

Grace's own tests were to be administered by Doctor McKirahan himself, but Thomas would be facing the papers in the examination hall alongside his fellow medical students.

There would be a practical component, too, and to pass the final examinations, the students would be required to provide diagnoses and treatments for any number of different diseases and ailments.

Grace listened sympathetically, and as they rode to her lodgings in a carriage, she told Thomas what she would do to help him.

"We'll study together," she said, and he looked at her in surprise.

"Really?" he said, and she nodded.

"Yes, whatever I don't understand, you'll explain, and whatever you don't understand, I'll explain," she replied.

He grinned at her and shook his head.

"What would I do without you, Grace?" he said, and Grace laughed.

"You don't need to do without me," she replied.

And so, for the next two days, they studied together, working day and night, their textbooks spread across the table in the lodgings Grace had taken for herself. They were visited several times by Lady Thornberry, who patiently sat and tested them on everything from the Latin names of tropical diseases to the treatment for whooping cough and the best way to set a broken bone.

"There, now, that's the last one. You did it, Thomas. You remembered them all," Lady Thornberry said, smiling as Thomas breathed a sigh of relief.

"Thank goodness. I thought I'd never do it. It's all so easy to forget," he said, and Grace smiled at him.

"You're a brilliant medical student, Thomas. Don't ever forget that," she said, and Thomas smiled.

"Not as brilliant as you," he replied.

Lady Thornberry had administered the same test to Grace, and she had remembered every name without a second thought, along with a dozen others not listed.

But there were still things she did not know–her anatomy was poor, her ability at mixing medicines was merely passable, and as for surgery...

"We both have things we're good at and things we're not so good at. That's why, when we open the hospital, we'll rely on one another," Grace said.

Her mother looked at her and shook her head.

"You're truly your father's daughter, Grace. No other young

lady, on inheriting an estate like Carshalton House, would think of giving it over to becoming a hospital," she said.

Grace blushed. She liked the idea of her father being proud of her, and she wondered what he would say if he had been there to see her take the medical examinations.

"But you think it's a good idea, don't you?" she said, and her mother nodded.

"I was doubtful at first. But the more I think about it, the more I know you're doing the right thing. I'm proud of you, Grace. Had you grown up with me, you wouldn't have done it, and it seems there's a reason for our separation, as painful as it's been," she replied.

Grace glanced at Thomas. To her surprise, he had fallen asleep, his head lolled to one side, his eyes closed, gently snoring. She smiled, and her mother rose quietly to her feet.

"Put a blanket over him. He's got a big day tomorrow," she whispered.

Grace fetched a blanket, returning to find Thomas fast asleep, his head rest on his textbook. She placed the blanket gently over him, running her hand over his hair, and smiling. Her mother watched her, and she looked up to find a tear running down Lady Thornberry's cheek.

"Are you all right, Mother?" she asked, and her mother nodded.

"Oh, yes. It's just… for a moment, you reminded me of your father and I. We fell in love when were very young. There were those who said it would never work, but we proved them wrong. We were so very in love, and I see that in the two of you. I'm so proud of you, Grace. You've become the very woman I imagined my daughter to be," she said, slipping her arm around Grace and kissing her on the cheek.

* * *

THE FIRST EXAMINATION was to take place at eight O'clock the following morning. Grace was awake early, but she allowed Thomas to sleep, only waking him when the time had come for them to leave.

He looked thoroughly embarrassed when he realised he had remained all night at her lodgings, but Grace had not had the heart to wake him, and her mother had told her let him sleep, lest disturbing him gave them both a restless night.

"Radius, Ulna Carpals..." he said, counting the names off on his fingers.

"You can't do anymore now," Grace said, and Thomas smiled.

"I know... but I can give the illusion of it, can't I?" he said.

They left Grace's lodgings, taking a carriage to the medical school, where a steady stream of students was now entering the examination hall. Thomas took a deep breath and smiled at Grace, who had been instructed to wait for Doctor McKirahan at the entrance to the library.

"Good luck," she said, putting her arms around him.

"And to you, too. I know you'll do well," he said, and she smiled.

"And I know you'll do well, too," she replied.

Grace watched as Thomas made his way inside, knowing he would excel, if only he believed he could do so. As he disappeared into the crowd, Doctor McKirahan appeared from the library, smiling, as he beckoned to her.

"Come along, Grace, it's time," he said, and she followed him into the library, past rows and rows of bookshelves, and up a flight of stairs to a door flanked by busts of Hippocrates and Galen.

"It's really very kind of you to arrange this, Doctor McKirahan," she said, but Doctor McKirahan shook his head and smiled.

"I think you're very brave, Grace, or foolhardy. Come along, let's begin," Doctor McKirahan said, and ushering her into the room, Grace was faced with a large desk, on which was laid half a dozen examination papers and a large, ticking clock.

"*This is it,*" she thought to herself, and she imagined Doctor Berkley and her father watching over her, as she sat down at the desk...

EPILOGUE

THE DOCTOR BERKLEY MEMORIAL
HOSPITAL

"*P*assed with flying colours," Doctor Mullen said, holding up Thomas's examination transcript.

Thomas breathed a sigh of relief, and Grace threw her arms around him, the two of them embracing in joy at the happiness of the moment they had waited so long for. It had been four weeks since the examinations had taken place, and having returned to Norfolk, Grace and Thomas been in a state of nervous excitement ever since.

"I knew you'd do it," Grace said, and Thomas grinned at her.

"I wouldn't have done if it hadn't been for you, Grace. You saved me," he exclaimed, but Grace shook her head.

"You're the one who sat the examinations, not me," she said, and now she turned expectantly to Doctor Mullen, who held her own results in his hand.

"I'm afraid whatever it says, it won't mean the same as Thomas's results. He'll receive his degree and become a doctor, but you'll only have your own knowledge of the results, Grace," he said, and Grace nodded.

She understood she could not be a doctor, but with the knowledge she had gained, and with Thomas's help, there was no reason why she should not put that knowledge to good use under the auspices of the new hospital.

As Doctor Mullen opened the envelope, she slipped her hand into Thomas's and held her breath. Doctor Mullen examined the letter, a smile coming over his face.

"Oh, Father, don't leave us in such suspense," Thomas exclaimed, his father laughed.

"Quite remarkable, Grace. You gained the highest marks of any student ever to sit the examinations – even your father," he said.

Grace's eyes grew wide with astonishment, and Thomas snatched the letter from his father's hands, staring at it in amazement.

"You passed everything, Grace – you didn't make a single mistake. And look what Doctor McKirahan's write – *Hippocrates himself could not have produced a finer set of results.* He's commended you to the faculty, and they're going to honour you with a degree," he said.

Grace could not believe what she was hearing. It was extraordinary, and she had to read through the letter a dozen times before she truly believed it. She had passed every exam and was commended in every subject from anatomy to tropical diseases.

"I can't believe it," she kept saying, and Thomas put his arms around her and kissed her.

"I can. You've worked hard your whole life long, Grace. You're the best doctor I know – begging your pardon, Father – and now you *can* be a doctor, not just a nurse," he said, but Grace shook her head.

"I want to be both – I want to have the skills of a doctor, and the care of a nurse. I want to show compassion and expertise, too. That's how I want it to be at the hospital," she said, and Thomas smiled at her.

"Let's go there now – you've got the keys. We can start

making plans," he said, and bidding Doctor Mullen goodbye, the two of them hurried out of the cottage, and through the woods, making their way up the ravine, past the churchyard, where Grace paused.

"I want to tell Doctor Berkley our good news," she said, and hurrying through the gate, she made her way amidst the long grass to the lichen covered memorial to her friend and mentor.

"He'd be proud of you, Grace," Thomas said, coming to stand next to her.

"I did it, Doctor Berkley – I did what I promised, and more," Grace said, reaching out and running her fingers along the stone.

At that moment, the sun came out from behind a cloud, and it was as though Doctor Berkley himself was smiling on them. As they left the churchyard, Grace glanced at the graves of Mary Carruthers and Lady Edith.

She was still uncertain about how she felt towards them, unsure how to remember them, even as she knew she would never again think of them as once she had.

"I suppose they taught me a great deal, and I can be thankful for that," she told herself, as she and Thomas headed in the direction of Carshalton House.

The gardens were overgrown, and the windows shuttered. The house was surrounded by memories, and yet standing before it, Grace saw possibility, too.

"We can do so much with it," Thomas said, and she nodded, slipping her hand into his.

"Imagine what it'll be like – the rooms filled with patients, the gardens tended to–a place for convalescence. Your father could have his own consulting room and laboratory, and you'll have one, too," Grace said, imagining everything they would achieve together.

"It's perfect. Everything 's perfect, except one thing," Thomas said, and Grace turned to him in surprise.

"But what's left? We've passed our exams, we've got the hospital, too. The wreckers are in prison..." she said, her words trailing off, as now he raised her hand to his lips and kneeled before her.

Grace's heart skipped a beat, and now he looked up at her with a gaze filled with love.

"Only to ask you to marry me," he replied.

But Grace did not need time to consider the question. She loved him, and there was no doubt in her mind as to the answer.

They were on the cusp of a new beginning, a whole lifetime lying before them, and she smiled at him, opening her arms as he rose to his feet.

"And I know just what I'm going to say," she replied, their lips meeting in a kiss—a kiss to seal the love they had found, the love to last the rest of their lives.

The End

If you enjoyed this story, could I please ask you to leave a review on Amazon?

Thank you so much.

Printed in Great Britain
by Amazon

30442768R00121